FEAR and TREMBLING

GHOLAM-HOSSEIN SA'EDI

FEAR and TREMBLING

GHOLAM-HOSSEIN SA'EDI

Translated, and with an Introduction
and a bibliography, by

MINOO SOUTHGATE

An Original by THREE CONTINENTS PRESS

3CP

© Minoo Southgate 1984

First Edition in English

Three Continents Press, Inc.
1346 Connecticut Avenue, N.W.
Washington, D.C. 20036

ISBN: 0-89410-287-7
ISBN: 0-89410-288-5 (pbk)
LC No: 81-51641

Cover Art by Tom Gladden

ACKNOWLEDGMENTS

I wish to thank Gholam-Hossein Sa'edi, Maryam Mafi, Donald Herdeck, and Edward M. Potoker for their assistance.

Minoo Southgate

INTRODUCTION

A. Modern Iranian Literature

"There is a kind of writer appearing with greater and greater frequency among us," says E. L. Doctorow, "who witnesses the crimes of his government against his countrymen. He chooses to explore the intimate subject of a human being's relationship to the state. His is the universe of the imprisoned, the tortured, the disfigured . . . ."[1]

These words could describe the majority of committed contemporary Iranian poets, writers, and playwrights who portray their countrymen as victims of oppression, tyranny, and political and bureaucratic corruption. The body of literature they have produced will surprise the Westerner whose notion of Iranian literature is based on scant examples of the poetry of Hafiz and Omar Khayyam celebrating wine, women, roses and nightingales. Today, committed Iranian writers use literature not to record their private reveries but to criticize and to reform their society.

The social commitment in modern Iranian literature is rooted in the struggle of the Iranian people for political and social change at the turn of this century. Literature exposed social and political wrongs and asked for their correction. Since the classic genres, being stylized and conventional in theme, vocabulary, and form, did not lend themselves to realistic portrayals of life, they were abandoned in favor of new literary forms. Both in content and form the poetry and fiction of the past seventy years broke with Persian classical literary tradition and turned to Western models instead.

In 1900 A.D. Iran's social and political structure still lingered in the Middle Ages. The struggle for reform, led by petit bourgeois classes, urban capitalists, intellectuals and the clergy, began late in the 19th century. As part of their effort to educate the public, the reformists used verse—the dominant literary form at the time—to point out social ills and to effect social change. While classical poetry had been, in the main, remote from everyday life, this new poetry was topical and pragmatic. Modern Iranian literature began when writers turned to contemporary events and to the lives of common people for their subject.

Writers and reformists found much to criticize. The autocratic Qajar dynasty (1794-1925), which had bankrupted Iran and placed it under British and Russian control, was itself a barrier to progress. The reformists, therefore, demanded a constitutional government. This they won in August 1906, but foreign and domestic problems continued to plague the country and corruption and injustice did not cease. The Qajar rule lasted until Reza Khan Pahlavi's coup d'état put an end to it in 1921.

Iran's social and cultural awakening in early 20th century led to a utilitarian view of literature: now the criterion for judging literature was whether it did anything for the people. The main literary form at this time was poetry, but the poetry of the constitutional movement broke from classical poetry. Stylized in language and conventional in imagery, classical poetry was addressed to a patron or to an elite class. It often dealt with the general and the universal rather than the specific, and failed to reflect the poet's contemporary society. By contrast, constitutional verse was in simple and often colloquial language, its audience was the man in the street, and its subject everyday issues and events. Though aesthetically inferior to classical poetry, constitutional verse was significant because it signaled a new phase in the history of Iranian literature: here, for its subject, literature drew upon life rather than a literary tradition. Since then, Iranian poets have explored ever new techniques and themes, but most remain socially committed. From Nima Yushij (1895-1959) to Ahmad Shamloo (b. 1925) and Reza Baraheni (b. 1935), Iranian poets have inspired their countrymen to fight oppression and to struggle for freedom and dignity.

Compared to poetry's eight decades of change, modern Iranian fiction has had a more difficult development, partly because for centuries prose had been neglected in favor of verse and partly because Persian prose had suffered a steady decline since the tenth century, becoming ornate, verbose, and formal. By the late 19th century, however, the introduction of printing and of European culture and literature had begun to contribute to the revitalization of prose, and literary reformists using European prose as their model, slowly narrowed the gap between prose and the spoken language. Effective journalistic prose had evolved from a colloquially influenced style by the early 1900s but it had not been imitated in early fiction whose dominant form in 1909-1932 was the escapist historical novel glorifying Iran's past. The Persian historical novel was influenced by mid-19th century French romantic literature.

Realistic Iranian fiction can be said to have begun in 1921 with the publication of Jamalzadah's collection of short stories *Once Upon a Time*. Jamalzadah (1895-1971), who had been educated in Europe, admired European literature, and especially the novel. Knowing that his countrymen esteemed poetry above prose, he pointed out in his introduction to his stories poetry's limitations in depicting everyday life and argued that realistic fiction required the more flexible medium of prose. Unfortunately, the development of fiction was hampered by the rule of Reza Shah (1921-1941), during which censorship forced most committed writers to cease writing. In the decade following Reza Shah's abdication in 1941, writers enjoyed freedom of expression. Mossadegh's premiership engendering new hope for freedom and democracy was ended in 1953 when Mossadegh was overthrown and the country was placed under military rule until 1957. Under the Shah, dissidents were ruthlessly suppressed and freedom of expression curtailed. Despite these restraints, however, modern Iranian writers were now independent enough to continue to work their way to a freer and more popular prose.

European and American literature, mostly in translation, contributed to the development of modern literature in Iran. Major French, Russian, English, and American writers began to appear in Persian editions in the fifties. In the sixties and seventies, in fact, translation of Western works formed about seventy-five percent of book publishers' literary output. In addition, the literary journals of the sixties and seventies (*Arash*, 1961-68; *Jung* [A Miscellany], 1965-68; *Payam-i Nuvin* [A New Message], 1958-68; *Rahnama-yi Kitab* [A Guide to Books], 1958-79; *Sukhan* (Word), 1943-80, and others) were publishing translations of Pound, Eliot, Faulkner, Steinbeck, Sartre, Apollinaire, Brecht, Lorca, Borges, and Yevtushenko, and introducing lesser-known writers to their audience. The introductions and critiques which often accompanied these literary works additionally provided guidance for the aspiring writers. Further, book reviews and discussions of theories of literature and genres contributed to the development of literary criticism in Iran betokening a growing intellectual interest in esthetics and the cultural role of the writer in modern society.

Modern drama, which had no native models to imitate, also began to emerge and to develop necessarily along European lines. Examples of Persian plays appeared gradually in the new literary journals.[2] Unfortunately, most of these journals were short-lived, or appeared only sporadically, because of financial problems, or censorship, or both. The same factors caused the more serious weeklies and newspapers to cease publication. Accordingly, some good work had been done and much ground had been cleared but the courageous struggle to maintain momentum and some semblance of independence in theme and style was always required.

Illiteracy and lack of public interest in serious literature were other factors that discouraged writers. Book circulation is and has been very low. A best-seller is a book that sells 3,000 copies and most works of course sell in the low hundreds. The authors (who get the usual ten or fifteen percent in royalties) receive little direct returns, and the typical writer works at a regular job to support himself, writing in his spare time.

But censorship, not economics, has been the committed writer's greatest bane. Under the Shah, as noted, artistic and intellectual freedom was sharply curtailed. To elude censorship, poets and writers resorted to esoteric writing, to allegory and symbolism. Their mood, however, relected in a literature that spoke of suffocation, alienation, isolation, loneliness, darkness and nothingness, made clear the subjective terrain of their perspectives and became to some degree the "substance" of the new fiction.

"Censorship has put all writers against the wall," Gholam-Hossein Sa'edi said in an interview with Richard R. Lingeman of *The New York Times*. He discussed the plight of Iran's independent writers who formed a writers' association "in order to conduct a legal . . . campaign against censorship and deal with common professional problems." The Association was harassed and its members were frequently imprisoned. The demands of the Writers Association were simple: "a place to meet, the right to publish a journal, no more censorship."[3]

Sa'edi described the censorship system as a "polycentric" system, "whereby government created professional and trade groups to ban works whose subject matter falls under their jurisdiction. Each new printing of a book must be approved, and the government will see what sort of an impact a book has before banning it."[4] Writers whose works met the disapproval of the Shah's censor agents were harassed, jailed, tortured, and even killed. As a writer who was jailed repeatedly, Sa'edi described his horror at discovering that whatever he wrote "could be interpreted (by censor agents) in thousands of different ways and with each new interpretation a new charge could be brought against" him.[5] He spoke of censorship's devastating effects on the writer:

The possibilities of being refused permission to publish or, even worse, being incarcerated, invades not only your waking hours but also your sleep, along with other nightmares. And the writer constantly thinks about how he would defend his characters against the unfounded charges of those ruthless prosecutors.[6]

In his books of prison poems, *Crowned Cannibals* and *God's Shadow*, poet and literary critic Reza Baraheni reveals his experiences in the Shah's prisons and torture rooms, where he was detained without due process, interrogated, flagellated, and threatened that his wife and daughter would be raped before his eyes unless he revealed certain information to his captors. "We have the tape of your speech in the States against the Shah, we have all the things you said about the White Revolution, and now we have a written document in the paper. We have all your books too, proof that your intention is to overthrow the rule of the Shah . . .," says Azudi, "the head executioner," who has strapped Baraheni to an iron bed. "But why don't you bring me to trial?" Baraheni says. "Don't you think that if you have all these documents against me, you can easily lock me up?"

"This is the court. There is no other court. I am the judge, the jury, the court, and the executioner . . . ," Azudi responds. Later he threatens, "I'll pull your tongue out of your mouth and I'll break your fingers one by one, so that you won't be able to write anything or say anything."

Saying this, he breaks the little finger of Baraheni's left hand.[7]

Under the Shah the majority of committed writers were jailed at least once. Not surprisingly, toward the end of the Shah's rule there was a marked reduction in publication of serious literary books.

The situation has only worsened following the 1979 revolution. Most writers who were forced into exile during the Shah's rule returned to Iran only to find the new regime more brutal than the Shah's. Some were jailed, some left Iran, others went underground. Disillusioned, thousands of intellectuals and students also have left the country. The fanatic mullahs demand uniformity and conformity. They label anything not to their liking *taquti*, a Koranic term meaning "misguided," and repress it ruthlessly. The Shah occasionally released jailed writers under pressure from Western human rights organizations; the mullahs have proven immune to any sort of pressure.

Currently, book publishing in Iran is limited to political, historical and religious materials whose purpose is to combat all Western influences and to justify the regime. In government-controlled newspapers, the mullahs exhort the faithful to vengeance and martyrdom, their atrocious Arabicized rhetorical prose reeking of blood and gore.

The mullahs, one of whose primary goals was the Islamization of education, have also done away with the academic freedom guaranteed in the 1906 Constitution. In September 1979, the Minister of Education declared that "only teachers whose Islamic credentials are verified by Islamic associations are qualified to continue in their profession."[8] Soon after, elementary and secondary school text-books were "changed to reflect the sectarian views of the ruling theocrats." Teachers and students were not allowed access to "additional reading material unless approved by the Islamic Association set up in all the schools." In the new curriculum instruction in the sciences and humanities was reduced in favor of compulsory religious indoctrination. Academic and intellecual freedom was further curtailed with the closure of the universities in 1980 and with the repeated purges of thousands of teachers and professors. The government also controls Iranian students abroad through a discriminatory allocation of foreign exchange. Since the spring of 1980, foreign exchange has been denied those students abroad who were studying "such subjects as humanities, economics, art, music, pure science, psychology and advanced medicine."

It is too soon to measure the effects of this period of intellectual and cultural repression on Iranian literature; but there is no doubt that the exile, imprisonment, torture, and execution of doctors, lawyers, students, teachers, professors, writers, artists, and all those who might show signs of thinking will have a terrible effect on the intellectual life of the country.

Sources:

Amnesty International Briefing, November 1967; Jalil Bahar, "The Theocrats Take Over," Index on Censorship, Vol. 10, No. 5, Oct. 1981, pp. 2-3; Muhammad-Taqi Bahar, Sabkshinasi (Tehran, 1948); Reza Baraheni, Crowned Cannibals (New York, 1977); God's Shadow: Prison Poems (Bloomington, 1976); and Tala dar Mis (Tehran, 1968); James Alban Bill, The Politics of Iran: Groups, Classes, and Modernization (Columbus, 1972); Edward G. Browne, A Literary History of Persia (Cambridge: Cambridge University Press, 1924); and The Press and Poetry of Modern Persia (Cambridge: Cambridge University Press, 1914); E.L. Doctorow, "The New Poetry," Harper's, May 1977, pp. 92-95; Nizam al-Islam Kirmani, Tarikh-i Bidari-yi Iranian (Tehran, 1966); Richard R. Lingeman, "Iranian Visitor," The New York Times, July 16, 1978, sec. 7, p. 31; Rouhollah K. Ramazani, "Iran: The Islamic Cultural Revolution," Change and the Muslim World

(Syracuse, 1981), pp. 40-48. Gholam-Hossien Sa'edi, "Thought: Manacled," *The New York Times*, July 21, 1978, p. 25; Leila Saeed, "Iran Since the Shah," *Index on Censorship*, Vol. 10, No. 3, June 1981, pp. 11-15. *Unsigned Article*, "I'lamiyah-yi Guruh-i Azadi-yi Kitab va Andishah," *Payam-i Danishju*, Shahrivar 1356 (Nov. 1976), pp. 51-94.

B. Gholam-Hossein Sa'edi: Life and Works

"If I had a *khirqah* (a traditional gown of Sufi masters) with which I were to vest someone after my death," Jalal Al-i Ahmad once wrote, "he would be Gholam-Hossein Sa'edi."[9] The author of social, political, and literary essays, several novels, anthropological monographs, and collections of short stories, Al-i Ahmad (1923-1969) emerged as a particular favorite of liberals and intellectuals in the 60's. His nationalistic views in *Gharbzadigi* (Westomania) were widely accepted by Iranian youths. A decade or so after Al-i Ahmad's sudden and suspicious death, Gholam-Hossein Sa'edi has indeed been vested with Al-i Ahmad's *khirqah* and his uncompromising integrity and courage has earned him the love and respect of the intelligentsia. Today he is Iran's most important writer, with over forty novels, collections of short stories, plays, film scripts, and anthropological monographs to his credit.

Sa'edi was born in 1935 in Tabriz, in the Northwestern province of Azerbaijan. An M.D. and a psychiatrist by training, he has first-hand knowledge of the sufferings of his people, especially the poor, and has successfully assimilated his experiences as a psychiatrist in his writing. Responding to the patriotic and nationalistic fervor stirred by Dr. Mossadegh, Sa'edi began writing in the early 1950's, when he was still a teenager. After the fall of Mossadegh, Sa'edi was briefly imprisoned. This was the first of at least sixteen instances of incarceration under the Shah, the last of which began in June 1974 and lasted until May 1975. He was tortured in jail and "forced to recant on television under threat that his aged mother would be killed."[10] His plight was publicized in the United States by the Committee for Artistic and Intellectual Freedom in Iran. In 1977 through the efforts of the Association of American Publishers' Freedom to Publish Committee, Sa'edi received an invitation to come to this country. He was denied a passport, however, and it was not until the summer of 1978, after pressure from human rights and writers' organizations, that Sa'edi was given permission to leave. At a news conference in the U.S., he spoke freely of "outrageous repression and censorship" which had "destroyed all forms of freedom of expression and publication in Iran."[11] He would not, however, consider living abroad. "I travel among people in the villages. All my ideas come from them. If I become disconnected from the people, my writing would be based only on memory," he said in an interview.[12] He met with several American writers and journalists, and in interviews and articles publicized the Shah's repressive policies. Returning to his homeland, however, he found the Ayatollah's Iran no more hospitable than the Shah's. To protect his safety, Sa'edi went underground and in the spring of 1982 was able to leave Iran for France.

Sa'edi's writing career began, as noted, in his late teens with the publication of short stories and articles in literary journals and periodicals. At twenty, he published his first collection of short stories. Later he worked as editor of several literary and cultural journals and magazines to which he contributed regularly. He was also one of the founders of the Writers Association, organized to protect writers and publishers against censorship and government harassment. Seven of his stories have been made into feature films for which he himself prepared the script. One film, "The Cow," based on a section of his novel *The Mourners of Bayal*, won an international film prize.[13] In the early and mid 1960's his plays were produced regularly and were shown on television. In the late 1960's, however, "the Ministry of Arts and Culture forbade the performances of his plays and later even persecuted some of the actors and actresses who had taken part in them."[14]

* * *

Sa'edi's works deal with interrelated sociopolitical and psychological problems. His characters come from a wide cross-section of Iranian society. Simple villagers, members of tribal societies, poverty-stricken ghetto-dwellers as well as middle class city residents are all represented in his writing. His political views are more accessible in his plays than in his fiction, which is often symbolic and surrealistic. *The Stick-Wielders of Varzil* (1965), *Five Plays about the Constitutional Revolution* (1966), *Dictation and Angle* (1968), *Cattle Fatteners* (1969), and *The Honeymoon* (1978) are overtly political. An allegory, *The Stick-Wielders of Varzil* condemns the superpowers' exploitation of minor countries. A group of villagers whose farms are plundered by wild boars are unsuccessful in getting rid of the animals. They go to an Armenian for help, and are given two hunters who get rid of the boars, but who refuse to leave the village and thus become a greater nuisance than the boars. The villagers seek the Armenian again and he lends them two new hunters to get rid of the first two. In the climactic conclusion of the play, the old and the new hunters join forces against the helpless villagers. In *Cattle-Fatteners*, a courageous journalist who is about to expose the corrupt dealings of an influential public figure is taken to a cattle-fattening farm, where he is kept prisoner and tempted with rich lamb stew and with the owner's wife. Failing to make him surrender, his captors have to kill him. This play "directs its attack at any institution, small or big, communist or capitalist, that would want to see its individuals castrated, bedded down, and fattened."[15]

The Honeymoon attacks police states and governments hostile to individualism. An old hag, the unlikely villain of this play, descends upon a honeymoon couple unexpectedly and, using force and intimidation, destroys their loyalty to each other. By the end of the play, she turns them into non-thinking machine-like creatures whose only concern is eating and drinking. Her mission accomplished, the old hag departs with the young husband, now an ally, and both go to new addresses and new victims.

Sa'edi means to educate the public through his plays. To this end, he often reduces complex socio-political problems to simple situations, making the message and meaning accessible to the least sophisticated audiences. The Western reader and theater-goer might find his plays too simple and obvious, but all levels of audiences in Iran admire Sa'edi's plays, which reflect their own problems, fears, disappointments, and mental aberrations.

Social criticism is prominent in Sa'edi's works about the middle and lower class city dwellers. His middle class characters are confused, alienated, nihilistic, aimless. They lack commitment and are plagued by vague fears and apprehensions. Their lives are precarious, frequently ending in madness and suicide. They have lost faith in traditional values without finding new values with which to replace the old. The colonel, his daughters, and his young second wife in "Calm in the Presence of Others" (1967) are good examples.[16] The colonel, whose thoughts give him no peace, drinks to get over his fears and to forget. But alcohol is no refuge and even sleep fails to bring him any peace. "I've never slept calmly or without some weird confused phantoms coming after me" (p. 100). Fear is a general affliction in Sa'edi's world. One of the colonel's daughters describes a patient at the hospital where she is a nurse: "Every day his eyes bugged out more than the day before, and the way he stared you'd think that something terrible was coming toward him, and that thing got so close that he got scared to death" (pp. 114-115). The characters see no purpose to their lives. "I feel so useless," complains the colonel's other daughter. "We're not like the old people and we're not like the young . . . . Some strange thing is killing me. I don't know what to do. I'm going mad" (p. 138). Another character complains about "the futile pointless way the world turns a man into garbage and excrement" (p. 134). For him, life, "the whole rat race, all that ranting and panting and milling around . . . the empty enthusiasm and excess" has led to a "cold, dead, icy existence . . . a perpetual idleness that's corrupted everything beyond hope . . ." (p. 133). We watch many of these characters fall to pieces and end in mental hospital wards, or in rented rooms dangling from a noose.[17]

Sa'edi's frenzied middle class world with its parties, cafés, and secret affairs constrasts with the bleak world of his poverty-stricken villagers and ghetto-dwellers. While the middle class characters begin with an appearance of hope and happiness, the lower class ones struggle in unrelieved misery. Starvation, ignorance, superstition, and physical and mental disease are constant in the world of "Dandil" (1968), "The Game Is Up" (1973), The Mourners of Bayal (1965), and Fear and Trembling (1968), among others. Islam, intertwined with superstition, plays a strong part in the life of the poor. The mosque is ever-present in Stick-Wielders of Varzil, Fear and Trembling, and The Mourners of Bayal. But neither the mosque nor the shrine of the Imam with its icons, banners, and votive candles, protects the believers from harm. The old women in The Mourners of Bayal weep for their village and resort to religion as well as witchcraft to divert the mysterious evil which threatens it. But nothing can save Bayal. The villagers go hungry, robbing their poor neighboring communities for food, suffering one disaster after another.

Poor city residents fare no better. The ghetto-dwellers in "The Game Is Up" live on little more than bread and water. The fathers often fail to find work, and the children scrounge in the trash for something to eat or to sell for a few pennies. Frustrated, the men abuse their wives and children. Life is cruel to the poor, and they are cruel to one another. Religion, a strong presence in their lives, is empty ritual and does not humanize them.

The father's abuse of the son, a frequent theme in contemporary Iranian fiction, is a central theme in "The Game Is Up," where son-killing and son-gagging become rituals in which all the adult males of the community participate. Sa'edi places this theme in a mythic context and sees it as a sort of reversed Oedipus complex.

Middle or lower class, Sa'edi's characters are paralyzed by an insidious fear which peoples their world with dangerous and elusive presences. As a psychiatrist who practiced in a poor district in Southern Tehran, Sa'edi had first hand knowledge of psychological traumas and disorders that afflicted his countrymen. "I'm afraid. I'm always afraid," Sa'edi quotes one patient in an article. "I'm afraid of sleep, too. I am arrested in my sleep and flagellated by all kinds of whips. After I wake up, I cannot walk for a long time. The soles of my feet are sore."[18]

This patient was a Tehran book seller who had been frequently arrested and tortured by the SAVAK. But the colonel in "Calm in the Presence of Others" and the villagers in *The Mourners of Bayal* and *Fear and Trembling*, though never jailed, are victims of similar fears. Sa'edi believes these disorders to be the result of life in a harsh environment, in an atmosphere of deprivation, tyranny and oppression. Many of Sa'edi's characters go mad. Some are taken to hospitals and to mental asylums. Few ever leave the hospital alive.

Sa'edi is a realist at heart although his work is often allegorical, symbolic, or surreal in its presentation. His style fluctuates between the realistic method of "The Game Is Up" and the allegorical and surrealistic modes, respectively, of *The Stick-Wielders of Varzil* and *The Honeymoon. The Mourners of Bayal* and *Fear and Trembling* employ a combination of all these styles. The more dominant the psychological disorder is in a character, the more surrealistic the work becomes, since the world of the story is seen through the character.

C. Fear and Trembling

Fear and Trembling (Tars va Larz), a novel in six sections or "Stories," was published in Tehran in 1968. Two years before, Tehran University had published Sa'edi's *People of the Wind (Ahl-i Hava)*, an anthropological monograph about the Persian Gulf coast, the area which serves as the setting of the novel. As fiction, *Fear and Trembling* can be appreciated independently of the anthropological study, but the monograph can enhance the reader's understanding of the novel's harsh Southern locale and the effects of this environment on the characters.

The anthropological monograph is based entirely on the author's experiences and observations in the area. It is not a methodical scientific study. It is, rather, an informal account by a compassionate observer who combines the sensitivity of the novelist and the skills of the psychiatrist in an effort to understand the coastal people and their culture.

To the Iranian city dweller this culture is almost as unfamiliar as it is to the Westerner. The Persian Gulf coast is geographically isolated from the rest of Iran and has been influenced by the customs, rituals, beliefs, and superstitions of Black Africa, India, and Arabia.[19] Africans (particularly those who were brought to the Persian coast from Somalia and Zanzibar and who have lived there for generations) have preserved their native heritage, and have strongly influenced the music, dance, and religion of the coastal people. At night, the spirit of Black Africa hovers over the coast, as the sound of the drum rises from every village and perhaps every shack.[20]

The bulk of *People of the Wind*, then, deals with religious rituals and beliefs which are for the most part the product of African influence. The coastal people (and the characters in *Fear and Trembling*) think themselves to be under constant threat from ubiquitous spirits (or winds—*badha*), which, they believe, can "ride" or "possess" human beings. The possessed person becomes ill and only a black shaman (male or female) can attempt to appease the spirit and persuade it to leave the victim's body. Once healed by the shaman, the possessed person becomes a member of "ahl-i hava," i.e., the "people of the wind." As stated earlier, the various myths, legends, and rituals, be they of Indian, Arabian, Islamic, or Persian origin, are intermixed. African chants, for instance, were replaced by Arabic verses in praise of the Prophet Mohammad and of Moslem saints, though the music and rhythms remained closer to the African base, and African rituals were modified in time to conform to Islamic practices.

The first and third "Stories" of *Fear and Trembling* show the influence of these beliefs and rituals on the lives of the coastal people. In the harsh, cheerless Southern locale, the fear of supernatural powers plays havoc with the inhabitants' lives, subjecting them to real and imagined ills. Seen through the villagers' eyes, the desert, the sea, the sun, the moon, and the sky appear ominous and full of foreboding. Elusive perils lurk in the villagers' paths, threatening their precarious peace and safety. The victims of hallucination and other mental aberrations, they are afraid of the dark, afraid even in their own homes.

In the first "Story" Salem Ahmad discovers an intruder in his house

xviii

and rushes to the conclusion that the intruder has the power to possess him and cause him to become ill. His conviction is so strong that moments after the encounter he falls ill and by the third day he is raving mad and has to be restrained in chains. The village shaman is called to cure him and to drive out the intuder, who, the villagers believe, could afflict them all.

To the reader, the intruder is merely a hungry black man, a cripple. But to the superstitious villagers he is an indestructible evil force. They feel justified in stoning the black man who, they believe, will rise again to afflict others as he has Salem. Ironically, superstition both causes the illness and effects the cure. Salem recovers when, as a last resort, the villagers lead him to the mound of rocks piled on the black man. The enemy's body thus becomes a shrine endowed with healing powers.

The victim of "possession" in the third "Story," however, is not as fortunate as Salem. Abd al-Javad's wife goes mad after a still-birth; and when the village women's home remedies fail to cure her, her husband takes her to Ishaq-i Hakim, or Isaac the Physician, a mysterious old man who lives in the outskirts of another coastal village. The husband is warned against "the greedy Jew," who "is not pure of heart," but he does not heed the warning, for he doubts that the village shaman can cure his wife. Isaac is in fact a quack whose only concern is money. The odd treatment to which he and his assistants (an old black couple) subject the patient proves fruitless and she dies. The episode ends with Isaac's jubilant departure for Jerusalem aboard a splendid ship which has come to fetch him. Like the Armenian in the *Stick Wielders of Varzil*, the Jewish physician in *Fear and Trembling* belongs to one of Iran's religious minorities. The Armenian and the Jew are disloyal to the people among whom they live; and, when asked for help, they do more harm than good. The Armenian is an ally of the hunters who plunder the village and his offer to help the villagers is motivated by greed and self-interest. Similarly, the Jewish quack has apparently stayed in the coast to fill his coffers, until he can obtain a passage to Jerusalem. The episode in *Fear and Trembling* may also have a political dimension. Written in the late 1960's, the episode could be an attack against Israel and her "seductive" offer of technological aid to the third world, especially Africa. Possibly, Sa'edi meant to suggest that Israel would provide no real aid and that the faith placed in her was unfounded, for Israel's loyalties lay elsewhere. Regardless of the validity of this interpretation, Sa'edi's choice of minority stereotypes to represent greed and disloyalty is unfortunate, especially when viewed in a broader context than that of Iranian villagers.

*   *   *

Like *Fear and Trembling*, *People of the Wind* depicts an inhospitable environment hostile to happiness and to mental and physical health. The heat is unbearable, the water scarce. In most areas drinking water is limited to rain water collected in exposed reservoirs and contaminated by parasites, dead animals, and insects. Well water is too salty to drink or to use in agriculture. The soil is too poor for farming or cattle-raising. The people subsist on wheat, dates and fish, but the primitive fishing gear and the small fishing boats they use make for a poor catch. Traditionally, therefore, the natives have lived as nomads or have travelled to Arab sheikdoms such as Dubai and Qatar as seasonal laborers. According to Sa'edi the Persian Gulf ports and towns have deteriorated in the past few decades and have suffered a decrease in population.[21] Even marriage and affairs of the heart are affected by economic factors. When fishing is good and the men have money, they marry; and when fishing is poor and their money runs out, they divorce their wives, who in turn go to date orchards to work at picking dates.[22]

The harsh, monotonous, cheerless life of the coastal area wearies the inhabitants. The land and the sea breed fear, anxiety, despair, and mental and emotional aberrations. The fear of hunger, the prevalence of disease and death, and the monotony of daily existence exhaust the inhabitants and drive them to deep states of depression and to isolation.[23]

A comparison of the novel and the monograph shows that Sa'edi patterned his fictitious setting and his characters after the real coastal villages he visited and the people among whom he travelled. Work is scarce in the village and some of the men have to travel to neighboring islands to find work. Some villagers cannot afford a wife at all; others can afford one for a few months each year. The sea and the land are stingy, and a meal of fish and dates counts as a feast.

Nor is there much chance for the villagers to improve their circumstances. In the fifth "Story" the villagers pool their resources and buy a motor launch to carry cargo between neighboring coastal villages. This enterprise, they hope, will avail them of year-round employment. On its maiden voyage, however, the launch is toyed with and driven about by a mysterious power. An ominous boat passes it by, manned by enigmatic figures clad in black. Like similar figures in *The Mourners of Bayal*, they foreshadow danger and doom. The village women's thanksgiving feast by the shore fails to assure the launch a safe journey. Far from its destination, the launch is sucked into a whirlpool.

In several episodes in the "Stories" the village is also adversely affected by intruders.[24] The intruder in the first "Story," already discussed, is an innocent black man whose presence, because of the villagers' superstitions and ignorance, inadvertently causes one man to go mad. In the second "Story" the intruder is a mullah, a representative of the clergy who frequent Iran's villages.[25] The mullah is dropped off in the village by a mysterious pick-up truck. The villagers respect the mullah and welcome him because he is a man of religion. They are also dazzled by his money and his show of learning. He marries the village's most sought-after woman and sets up house briefly, until the mysterious pick-up returns and takes him away. Shortly thereafter, his wife gives birth to a monstrous child and both she and the baby die moments later. The mullah, we realize, has left for other villages and similar visitations. In this episode Sa'edi's criticism is directed at Moslem clergy who, like the mullah, feel entitled to the best of everything and who abuse the people's trust. The episode is especially poignant today, in light of the mullahs' dominion and of Ayatollah Khomeini's reign of terror in Iran. In the words of French critic Jérome Dumoulin, "cette nouvelle . . . semble anticiper [la noce fatale] de la jeune Perse et du vieil ayatollah."[26]

The intruder in the fourth "Story" is a child who is found in the outskirts and brought to the village, where it causes strange incidents and disrupts the villagers' lives. We have once again the evidence of the pervasive fear of the stranger and the stranger's possible evil powers. But the symbolism is difficult to decode. The child is found striding by the shore, a shinbone tucked under its arm. It has translucent skin and eyes of different color which grow larger as the story progresses. The relation established between the child and the sea, the child and the wind, and the child and the gypsies is not explained. Although the episode remains enigmatic, such loose ends are part of the technique of Fear and Trembling: The Six "Stories" run from six to seventeen sections, each section containing a separate episode. Some episodes include strange incidents that are never explained or taken up again. This technique is successful in the majority of the "Stories," where the episode's main idea is clear and the incident, though unexplained, contributes to the theme. The loose ends in the fourth "Story," however, do not seem to add up.

The novel's most sinister intruders are Westerners who appear in the climactic episode in the sixth "Story." They arrive in a magnificent ship and camp outside the village. Their presence starts a degradation of the villagers who stop fishing and who become contemptuous of their own way of life. Once kind and helpful to one another, they become suspicious and self-centered. Greedy for material possessions, the villagers rob the strangers and amass useless articles, or objects whose utility is unknown to them. Their moral deterioration is accompanied by a physical metamorphosis as the strangers' rich but indigestible food turns them into obese bloated creatures no longer resembling humans. The strangers' sudden departure forces the villagers to rob one another for food, since they are no longer fit to fish and to resume their old way of life. Armed with knives and hatchets, in the sinister ending of the novel, the villagers chase one another into dark alleys, with murder in their hearts.

The intruders in this episode represent Westerners who introduce underdeveloped countries to advanced technology. The episode suggests that although the presence of Western technology may initially improve the lives of the people, it ultimately does them more harm than good. If the underdeveloped nation does not master the technology (in the novel the villagers amass objects the use of which is unknown to them) it has to remain dependent on the West to run its industry and economy.[27] In addition to creating dependency, contact with the West causes moral dislocation, as Western values weaken native mores. Often the underdeveloped nation grows contemptuous of its way of life and blindly imitates the West. Social and economic chaos results when the West is eventually forced to leave.

The concluding episode of *Fear and Trembling* reflects the material prosperity of the last years of the Shah's reign and foreshadows the aftermath of the 1979 revolution. In the 1970s huge increases in the oil revenues brought riches and prosperity to many Iranians. Determined to turn Iran into a world power, the Shah began a massive industrialization plan. Farmers and peasants flocked to the cities to work in factories. To share in the oil wealth, foreign businessmen, advisors, technicians, contractors, and companies went to Iran. Rapid economic and social change combined with discontent caused by economic inequality, by repression, and by the Shah's indifference to Islamic mores led to the revolution. The technicians and advisors left Iran, the process of industrialization came to a halt, and the economy fell into disarray. Sa'edi's murderous villagers in *Fear and Trembling's* concluding episode resemble the rival political and religious factions of post-revolution Iran.

*   *   *

Structurally *Fear and Trembling* resembles *The Mourners of Bayal*, which preceded it by three years. Both combine the techniques of the novel and the short story. Both are divided into sections, or "Stories," which are self-contained though related to the rest and enriched by them. The stories share the same cast of characters, although each story centers around a different character or group of characters. Reflecting the linguistic and intellectual limitations of the villagers, the dialogue is very simple; at times, childish and repetitious. In both books, mysterious events cause life to go from bad to worse. Death, symbolized by the coffin in *Fear and Trembling* and by the mortuary slab in *The Mourners of Bayal*, makes a perpetual presence in both works.

The Mourners of Bayal ends with the ominous image of sick horses by the village pool.

> *Their heads hanging over the pool, their mouths half open, clotted maroon blood foamed from their gullets, plopped into the pool, and came to life, like tadpoles and frogs which had made their way out of a dark narrow sewer and had reached a slimy pool.*

Still more sinister, the climactic episode of *Fear and Trembling* ends with breach of loyalty among neighbors and friends who have become hateful, violent, and suspicious of each other.

> *In the shadow of the walls, Kadkhoda's son, an old hatchet in his hand, tiptoed toward Mohammad Hajji Mostafa. The moon over the Ayyub reservoir had burned itself out, extinguishing itself in the dark, prolonged night.*

Minoo Southgate
Baruch College, CUNY

FOOTNOTES

[1] "The New Poetry," *Harper's*, May 1977, p. 92.

[2] There is no evidence that secular drama ever existed in Iran. Persian native drama was limited to *ta'ziyah*, or passion plays, dealing with the lives of Moslem saints and martyrs.

[3] "Iranian Visitor," *The New York Times*, July 16, Sec. 7, p. 31.

[4] Ibid.

[5] "Thought: Manacled," *The New York Times*, July 21, p. 25.

[6] Ibid.

[7] *God's Shadow: Prison Poems* (Bloomington, 1976), pp. 18–19.

[8] All references in this paragraph are to Jalil Bahar, "The Theocrats Take Over," *Index on Censorship*, Vol. 10, No. 5, Oct. 1981, pp. 2—3. See also Leila Saeed, "Iran Since the Shah," *Index on Censorship,* Vol. 10, No. 3, June 1981, pp. 12—15; and Ruhollah K. Ramazani, "Iran: Islamic Cultural Revolution," *Change and the Muslim World* (Syracuse, 1981), pp. 40—48.

[9] Quoted by Massud Farzan, *Books Abroad*, Summer 1974, p. 624.

[10] Richard R. Lingeman, "Public Pressure," *The New York Times*, Feb. 12, 1978, Sec. 7, p. 35.

[11] "Iranian Author Charges Repression Is Continuing," *The New York Times*, June 18, 1978, p. 28, col. 1.

[12] Richard R. Lingeman, "Iranian Visitor," *The New York Times*, July 16, 1978, sec. 7, p. 31.

[13] For Persian titles and for publication data see the bibliography of Sa'edi's works following this introduction.

[14] Nithal Ramon, "Profile: Gholam Hoseyn Sa'edi," *Index on Censorship*, Vol. 7, No. 1, Jan—Feb. 1978.

[15] Massud Farzan, *Books Abroad*, Summer 1974, p. 168.

[16] A novella published in a collection of short stories entitled *Nameless and Elusive Apprehensions*. All references are to Robert Campbell's translation of the novella in *Dandil: Stories from Iranian Life* (New York: Random House, 1981). Page numbers are given in parentheses.

[17] See the plays "Invitation," in *House of Light* (1967) and *Two Brothers* (1968).

[18] "Thought: Manacled," *The New York Times*, July 21, 1978, p. 25, col. 2.

[19] For generations the coastal people have sailed to the shores of Africa, India, and Arabia to earn a living.

[20] *People of the Wind*, p. 6.

[21] For a detailed account of this deterioration and its causes see *People of the Wind*, pp. 13—17.

[22] Ibid, p. 17.

[23] Ibid, pp. 21 ff.

[24] The intruder is a recurrent figure also in Sa'edi's plays. See, for example, *The Honeymoon* and *Stick-Wielders of Varzil.*

[25] See also Sa'edi's mullah in the novel *Cannon* (1968).

[26] "Nouvelle: les avertissements des poètes persans," *L'Express,* du 9 au 15 août, 1980, p. 34.

[27] The Third World's ignorance of Western technology is the theme of the sixth section in *The Mourners of Bayal.* Here the villagers find a large rectangular metal box and decide that it is a tomb belonging to a holy shrine. They carry it to a hill top with their sacred icons and banners, and they build a wall around them all. The village sick and crippled are then chained to the box to be healed. Soon after, the box, apparently a generator, is retrieved by an American officer who callously knocks down the shrine and tramples the sacred objects in it. See 'Abd al-Ali Dastghayh, *Naqd-i asar-i Ghulamhusayn Sa'idi,* 3rd ed. (Tehran: Chapar, 1352/1973), pp. 39 ff.

GHOLAM-HOSSEIN SA'EDI:
A BIBLIOGRAPHY

The Library of Congress transliteration system has been followed, with the exclusion of diacritical marks.

I. Area Studies

Ahl-i hava. Tehran: Intisharat-i Mu'assisah-yi Mutali'at-i Ijtima'i, No. 36, 1345/1966.
Ilkchi. Tehran: Danishkadah-yi Adabiyat, Intisharat-i Mutali'at va Tahqiqat-i Ijtima'i, No. 15, Daftarha-yi Munugrafi, No. 5, 1342/1964.
Khiyav ya Mishkin Shahr: Ka'bah-yi yaylaqat-i Shahsavan. Tehran: Intisharat-i Mu'assisah-yi Mutali'at va Tahqiqat-i Ijtima'i, No. 30, 1344/1965.

II. Fiction

'Azadaran-i Bayal (8 connected stories). Tehran: Nil, 1343/1965.
Dandil: majmu'ah-yi dastan (stories: "Dandil," " 'Afiyatgah," "Atish," "Man va kachal va Kaykavus"). Tehran: Amir Kabir, 2536/1977.
"Du baradar" (story), *Arash*, 1:5 (Azar 1341/1962), 71-85.
"Gida" (story), *Sukhan*, 13:8 (Azar 1341/1962), 834-44.
"Gumshudah-yi lab-i darya" (story), *Arash*, 2:14 (Bahman 1346/1967), 33-49. (This is the 4th story in the collection *Tars va Larz*.)
Gur va gahvarah (stories: "Zanburak khanah," "Sayah bah sayah," "Ashghalduni"). Tehran: Agah, 2536/1977.
"Murgh-i anjir" (story), *Sukhan*, 7:4 (Tir 1335/1956), 372-377.
Shabnishini-yi bashukuh (stories: "Shabnishini-yi ba shukuh," "Chatr," "Marasim-i murafi'ah," "Khwabha-yi pidaram," "Hadisah bikhatiri farzadan," "Zuhr kah shud," "Mufattish," "Dayirah-yi darguzashtigan," "Sarnivisht-i mahkum," "Maskharah-yi navankhanah," "Majlis-i tawdi' "). Tehran: Amir Kabir, 1350/1972.
"Shafayaftah'ha" (story), *Sukhan*, 14:4-5 (Mihr-Aban 1342/1963), 412-27. (This is the 2nd story in the collection, *'Azadaran-i Bayal*.)
"Shafa-yi 'Ajil" (story), *Arash*, 2:5 (Azar 1345/1966), 28-34. (This is the

3rd story in the collection *Tars va Larz*.)

· *Tars va Larz* (6 connected stories), Tehran: Kitab-i Zaman, 1347/1968.

Tup (novel). 2nd ed. Tehran: Ashrafi, 1347/1968.

Vahimah'ha-yi binam va nishan (stories: "Du baradar," "Si'adatnamah," "Tab," "Aramish dar huzur-i digaran"). Tehran: Nil, 1346/1967.

III. Plays, Film Scripts, and Pantomimes

(Sa'edi's plays are published under the pen name Gawhar Murad.)

'Aqibat-i qalamfarsa'i (plays: " 'Aqibat-i qalamfarsa'i," "In bah an dar"). Tehran: Agah, 1354/1975.

" 'Arusi" (play), *Arash,* 1:3 (Urdibihisht 1341/1962), 17-24.

A-yi bi kulah, a-yi ba kulah (play). 5th ed. Tehran: Agah, 2537/1978.

Bamha va zir-i bamha (play). Tehran: no publisher, 1340/1961.

Bihtarin baba-yi dunya (play). Tehran: Shafaq, 1344/1965.

Chashm dar barabar-i chashm (play). Tehran: Amir Kabir, 1350/1971.

Chub bidastha-yi Varzil (play). Tehran: Murvarid, 1344/1965.

Dah lalbazi (pantomimes: "Pupak-i siyah," "Dasht payma," "Faqir," "Da'vat," "Zulamat," "Shafa'at," "Ziyafat," "Shahadat," "Jangal," "Tali' "). Tehran: *Arash,* 1342/1963.

Diktah va zaviyah (plays: "Diktah," "Zaviyah"). Tehran: Nil, 1347/1968.

"Faqir" (pantomime), *Sukhan* 13:11-12 (Isfand 1341-Farvardin 1342/1963), 1177-78.

Fasl-i gustakhi (film script). Tehran: Nil, 1348/1969.

Gav (film script). Tehran: Agah, 1350/1971.

"Intizar" (pantomime), *Arash,* 2:1 (Tir 1343/1964), 111-14.

Janishin (play). 3rd ed. Tehran: Agah, 2537/1978.

"Khanah'ha ra kharab kunid" (play), *Arash,* 1:7 (Winter 1342/1964), 3-33.

Kalatah gul (play). Tehran: no publisher, 1340/1961.

Karbafak'ha dar sangar (play). Tehran: Kitabfurushi-yi Tehran, 1339/1960.

Khanah rawshani (plays: "Khanah rawshani," "Da'vat," "Dast-i bala-yi dast," "Khusha bihal-i burdbaran," "Payam-i zan-i dana"). Tehran: Ashrafi, 1346/1967.

"Laylaj" (play), *Sukhan,* 8:8 (Azar 1336/1957), 800-803.

Ma nimishinavim (play). Tehran: Amir Kabir, 2537/1978.

Mah-i 'asal (play). Tehran: Amir Kabir, 2537/1978.

Panj nimayishnamah az inqilab-i mashrutiyyat (plays: Az pa nayuftadah'ha," "Gurgha," "Nanah Unsi," "Khanah'ha ra kharab kunid,"

"Bamha va zir-i bamha"). Tehran: Ashrafi, 1345/1966.
Parvarbandan (play). Tehran: Nil, 1348/1969.
"Qasidakha" (play), *Sadaf*, 6 (1338/1959).
"Shaban faribak" (play), *Sadaf*, 10 (1340/1961).
"Shahadat" (pantomime), *Arash*, 1:5 (Azar 1341/1962), 5-8.
Vay bar maghlub (play). Tehran: Nil, 1349/1970.
"Ziyafat," "Faqir," and "Az pa nayuftadah'ha" (pantomimes and play),
   Arash, 1:6 (Khurdad 1343/1964), 34-57.

IV. Miscellaneous

"Gujah dur, bakh gujah dur" (reflections on Samad Bihrangi's life and
   death), *Arash*, 2:5 (Azar 1347/1968), 15-16, 106-107.
Sad dar: barguzidah az nivishtah'ha-yi Zand va Pazand (trans. of Pahlavi
   texts). Tehran: 1337/1958.

V. Sa'edi's Works in English Translation

Dandil: Stories from Iranian Life ("Dandil," "The Game Is Over,"
   "Keykavus, Baldy and Me," "Calm in the Presence of Others," "The
   Rubbish Heap"), trans. Robert Campbell, Hasan Javadi, and Julie
   Scott Meisami. New York: Random House, 1981.
"The Game Is Up," in *Modern Persian Short Stories,* trans. and ed. Minoo
   Southgate. Washington, D.C.: Three Continents Press, 1980.
"The Wedding," trans. Jerome W. Clinton, *Iranian Studies,* 8:1-2 (Winter-
   Spring 1975), 2-47.

VI. Literary Criticism on Sa'edi

English items are asterisked.

Anvari, Hasan. (Review of *A-yi bi kulah, ay-i ba kulah*), *Rahnama-yi
   Kitab* (July 1968), 171-73.
Dastghayb, 'Abd al-Ali. *Naqd-i asar-i Ghulamhusayn Sa'edi.* 3rd ed.
   Tehran: Chapar, 1352/1973.
*Farzan, Massud. (Review of *Parvarbandan*). *Books Abroad* (Winter
   1972), 167-68.
* _____ (Review of *Gur va gahvarah*). *Books Abroad* (Summer
   1974), 624-25.
Hisami, Hushang. (Review of *Ay-i bi kulah, ay-i ba kulah*). *Arash,* 2:2

(Isfand 1346/1968), 107-10.

Ibrahimi, Nadir. "Bazdid-i qissah'ha-yi imruz," *Payam-i Nuvin*, 8:8 (Bahman 1345/1966), 82.

Kiyanush, Mahmud *Barrasi-yi shi'r va nasr-i mu'asir dar asari az Jalal Al-i Ahmad, Sadiq Chubak, Darvish, Akbar Radi, Ghulamhusayn Sa'idi, Muhammad Riza Shafi'i Kadkani, Siyavush Kasra'i, Jamal Mirsadiqi*. Tehran, 1353/1974.

Parham, Sirus. (Review of "Qasidakha" and "Shaban Faribak"), *Rahnama-yi Kitab* (April 1961), 21-22.

*Ramon, Nathil. "Profile: Gholam Hoseyn Sa'edi," *Index on Censorship*. 7:1.

S.T. (Review of *Bamha va zir-i bamha*), *Arash*, 1:3 (Urdibihisht 1341/ 1962), 90-92.

*Yar Shater, Ehsan. "The Modern Idiom," *Iran Faces the Seventies*. New York: Praeger, 1971, pp. 312-14.

FEAR and TREMBLING

FIRST STORY

The sun was at its zenith when Salem Ahmad woke up. It was already sultry. Instead of cool morning air, hot air billowed into the room through the ventilation tower. Salem Ahmad rose, swept up his headcloth by the wall and wrapped it around his head. He went into the bath, picked up the empty buckets, and went out to the porch. There he waited until his eyes were used to the intense midday sun; then, putting the buckets down, he rolled his bicycle, which had been leaning against a *konar* tree, into the shade. He unwound the rope from the carrying rack and, tying the buckets behind the saddle, he put on his clogs and walked the bike across the courtyard, looking at his chest, the bicycle, and his legs reflected in the dark windows of the winter rooms.*

Near the courtyard door he heard an unfamiliar cough. He stopped and listened. The cough was repeated, followed by a strange sound, something like that of a broken oar dipping into the water.

Salem Ahmad looked around him. The *konar* branches were moving; a shadow seemed to be lurking in between the leaves. Salem Ahmad stepped back, then, getting hold of himself, he started for the outside. About to leave the courtyard, he suddenly caught sight of the parlor door, half open. He stopped and listened; nothing. He wondered who had opened the door. No one had entered the parlor for years. He tiptoed to the door slowly. The room was dark, but a shaft of sunlight lit the threshold through the half-opened door. Salem Ahmad mumbled a prayer and dashed out of the courtyard door. Outside, there was Mohammad Hajji Mostafa's cow eating garbage. On the shore the rowboats lay side by side, shadows bouncing about them, the fishing nets spreading in the hot noon sun, stirring as if alive.

Salem Ahmad leaned his bicycle against his neighbor's porch and looked around him in terror. The door and windows of the parlor were open on the street side. Salem Ahmad was convinced that someone was in the room.

* Well-sunned rooms used during the winter months.

He went towards the parlor with unsure steps, and so did his shadow. A pleasant scent came from the room. Salem heard his name being called from the sea. He turned and looked behind him; nothing! Only a boat the size of a matchbox was pinned against the horizon. He rose on his toes gingerly, stretched his neck and glanced inside the parlor from the edge of the window.

A tall, thin black man with a very small head was sitting beside the open fire. He was wearing a long galabiya. He had one wooden leg stretched out beside the fire; the other, the good one, was folded beneath him. The Black was holding the parlor's big coffee pot over the fire as the room filled with the strong aroma of coffee. Salem Ahmad leaped back and dashed toward the houses on the far side of the square, forgetting the bicycle.

2

Saleh Kamzari was still asleep on the floor in the bath when Salem Ahmad burst in. Saleh pushed the headcloth off his face and opened his eyes.

"What's the matter, Salem?" he asked.

"Hey, Saleh, get up! Hurry up, get up!" said Salem Ahmad.

"What's the matter, Salem? What's happened to you?" said Saleh Kamzari, sitting up.

Saleh sat in the doorway, gathering in his hand the old towel which hung before the door in place of a curtain.

"I was going to fetch water from the reservoir when he possessed me," he said.*

"Possessed you? Where? How?"

"First I heard him cough. My arms and legs went numb and I couldn't move. I thought he was up the tree, but he wasn't."

"Where was he then? In the bath?"

"No, he wasn't in the bath, either."

"He possessed you at the well, then?"

"God have mercy! I wouldn't go near the well this time of day!"

Startled, Saleh sat closer, facing Salem Ahmad.

* Salem Ahmad believes himself to be possessed by a supernatural force embodied by the black man.

"O Mohammad, Prophet of God! Then where was he?" he said.

"He was sitting in the parlor," said Salem Ahmad.

"Sitting in the parlor?" Saleh said, rising to his knees.

"I swear I'm not lying. He was sitting by the fire, making coffee."

"God have mercy on us!" said Saleh Kamzari.

"What shall I do, Saleh? I'm feeling very ill. My body is getting stiff as a board," Salem said, beginning to shiver.*

"Do you want me to fix you the waterpipe?" asked Saleh.

"Would it do me any good?"

"Of course. The smoke will help you feel better. It's good for everything."

"All right then. Maybe the tobacco will restore me."

Saleh Kamzari left the bath. Trembling with fear, Salem Ahmad looked at the four corners of the bath and its empty, rusted out buckets by the wall. He saw small shadows moving inside the buckets. Breaking into a cold sweat, he cautiously crawled out of the bath, fleeing into the next room. There, the sun was spilling through the ruined walls of the ventilation tower above, flooding over the dirt floor. The inverted bell-type mouth of the shaft sucked in the sound of the sea, blowing it into the room below.

Saleh Kamzari returned with the waterpipe and put it before Salem Ahmad.

"Smoke, Salem."

"May God help me! My heart is full of fear."

"He will. He will."

They fell silent. Salem Ahmad finished smoking and the two walked out of the room.

"Can you see, Saleh?" Salem asked.

"See what?"

"My house—I mean the parlor."

"Not too well."

"What should we do now?"

"I don't know."

"I'm going to die of fright. I can't go near the house."

"You shouldn't go home, Salem Ahmad. We'd better tell the others what's happened."

They walked down the garbage-strewn path to the mosque.

"Sit down here. I'll take care of the rest."

* Sometimes the victim of the supernatural power is afflicted with a complete stiffness of the body.

Salem Ahmad sat on the ground, his head hanging over his chest. Saleh climbed on top of the coffin and cried out.

"There is no God but Allah, and Mohammad is Allah's messenger."*

The villagers heard Saleh's cry and thought someone had died. Doors swung open and the men dashed out, their headcloths in their hands.

3

The village men gathered outside Kadkhoda's** house and sat together at the door.

"This isn't something we can resolve; we'll have to send for Zahed," Kadkhoda said.

"I don't think Zahed is in his shack this time of day," Mohammad Hajji Mostafa said.

"O Merciful God! I hope he is," Salem Ahmad moaned.

"How do you know he isn't there? Let's send someone after him," Zakariya said.

"Who have we got to send?" Saleh said.

"Mohammad Ahmad Ali can go fetch him," Abd al-Javad said.

"What if he's asleep?" said Mohammad Ahmad Ali.

"Wake him and tell him to come here," said Zakariya.

Mohammad Ahmad Ali walked between the rows of houses till he reached the Ayyub reservoir. Then, turning, he passed the ruins of the house of the late ship captain Bin Ali, and reached Zahed's shack. The curtain door was dropped and there was no sound anywhere. Mohammad Ahmad Ali coughed. No one answered.

"Zahed! Hey, Zahed!" Mohammad Ahmad Ali called aloud.

"Hey, Mohammad Ahmad Ali, come in," Zahed called from inside.

Mohammad Ahmad Ali pushed the curtain aside and went in. Zahed was sitting on a mat, mixing *kiliya**** and tobacco.

"Hello, Zahed."

"Hello, Mohammad Ahmad Ali. Come in," said Zahed without raising his head.

---

*The formula recited is the *ashhad* (I testify). It is the creed of the Mohammedans. The village coffin, kept at the mosque, recurs later in the stories.

** "Kadkhoda" is a title given to the head of a village.

*** A narcotic.

Mohammad Ahmad Ali sat down, took a pinch of *kiliya* and put it behind his cheek. Zahed took some, too, and swallowed the juice.

"How is it? It's good *kiliya*, isn't it?" said Zahed.

"It's very hot and very good."

"An Indian beggar sold it to me."

"What did you give him in return?"

"A bamboo stick."

"That was a good deal." Mohammad Ahmad Ali took some *kiliya* and tied it in a knot in the corner of his headcloth.

"I'd run out of *kiliya*, but I had plenty of bamboo sticks," Zahed said.

Mohammad Ahmad Ali turned around and looked at Zahed's drums, incense burners, and bamboo sticks.

"When I go to sea, my legs swell. The sea has turned against me," said Zahed.

"The sea has turned against everybody. Why has it, Zahed?"

"I've no idea. That's the sea for you. Sometimes she's good; sometimes she's bad. Sometimes she's your friend, sometimes your enemy."

Mohammad Ahmad Ali remained silent, watching Zahed crumble the *kiliya* between his dark, long fingers.

"Hey Mohammad Ahmad Ali, didn't you find Zahed?" Suddenly Zakariya called from behind the shack.

Zahed recognized his voice.

"Come in, Zakariya. I've got some good *kiliya*," he said.

"Hey, Mohammad Ahmad Ali, did you come here to call Zahed or to chew *kiliya*?" he asked, then turned to Zahed. "Hey, Zahed, come here a minute. The men are waiting for you."

Zahed got up, picked his headcloth, which lay over a drum, and left the shack with Mohammad Ahmad Ali. The village men were waiting at the Ayyub reservoir.

"Where have you been, wild man?* Everybody's waiting here in this heat and you can't bring yourself to come out a minute," cried Mohammad Hajji Mostafa, who was standing behind the rest.

"I'm at your service. I've got *kiliya,* enough for everybody," Zahed said, laughing.

"Come and take a look at this poor soul," said Saleh Kamzari, pointing at Salem Ahmad.

"What's the matter?" said Zahed, surprised.

"He's been possessed. It happened an hour ago," said Saleh.

"You're joking?" laughed Zahed.

*In the Persian, *jangali.*

"No, I'm not. Who would feel like joking this time of day?" said Saleh Kamzari.

Zahed went over to Salem Ahmad, who was lying on the ground. The men fell silent. Zahed bent over and took Salem Ahmad's hands in his. Saleh Kamzari and Mohammad Hajji Mostafa were crouched, one on each side of Zahed. Far off, there was a commotion. Something seemed to be howling Salem's name from the sea.

4

The men returned and gathered behind the mosque.

"Haste makes waste. We've got to wait a little and see what happens," said Zahed.

"How long, then, should we wait?" Mohammad Hajji Mostafa asked.

"Zahed is in charge here. We've got to do as he says," responded Zakariya.

Zahed sat down at Salem Ahmad's head.

"Hey, Salem Ahmad, tell me all about it. I want to know what it was like," he said.

"I don't know what I saw, Zahed. I just saw it for a second," Salem said.

"Well, what was it like?" Zahed asked.

"Don't ask. If I start telling you my whole body will grow stiff like a board," said Salem.

"Well, in that case don't," said Zahed, turning to the men.

"The stranger must possess an evil power.* He could afflict the rest of us."

Salem began to tremble.

"What are you going to do with the stranger, Zahed?" asked Mohammad Ahmad Ali, who was standing behind the rest.

"We've got to drive him out," said Zahed.

"How can we do that?" asked Kadkhoda.

"Not us. Only Zahed can handle him," said Zakariya.

"I'm scared! I'm scared!" Mohammad Ahmad Ali said with a trembling voice.

"No one has any reason to be scared, except for Salem Ahmad, who has been possessed. Let everybody keep his chin up, or we'll all become

*In the original, mazarrati, i.e., a supernatural power that harms the subject it "rides" and which usually cannot be appeased.

possessed and fall ill," said Zahed.

"Did you hear, Mohammad Ahmad Ali? Did you hear what Zahed said? He said we shouldn't panic or lose our heads," Zakariya shouted.

"What are you going to do, Zahed? Beat the drum?" asked Saleh Kamzari.

"If he wants to beat the drum I'll fetch it," said Abd al-Javad.

"You're not supposed to beat the drum this time of day," said Zahed.

"What should we do then?" said Zakariya.

"Wait here until it's night," Zahed said.

"That's right. I won't do anything until it gets dark. Anyone who wants to leave, can. Salem Ahmad will stay. I'll stay and anyone else who wants to, will stay," Zahed said.

"When should we come back?" Saleh asked.

"Come back when it gets dark," advised Zahed.

The men rose. Salem, Zahed and Mohammad Ahmad Ali stayed behind. Mohammad Ahmad Ali untied the knot in his headcloth and took the *kiliya* out. Zahed took a pinch and put it behind his cheek.

"Take some. It's good for you," he said to Salem.

"I'm scared. I'm sick with fright," Salem Ahmad said.

"You'll feel better if you chew some," Zahed asserted.

"It's very hot and very good. Zahed bought it from an Indian beggar," agreed Mohammad Ahmad Ali.

Salem Ahmad put a pinch of *kiliya* behind his cheek, while fearfully watching the sky flame up. It was still a long time before night.

Mohammad Hajji Mostafa's cow went around the square and entered an alley. Suddenly Salem Ahmad trembled violently and vomited. He was paralyzed with fear. Zahed stretched him on the ground. Then, with the help of Mohammad Ahmad Ali, Zahed dragged the coffin over and set it alongside Salem Ahmad, sheltering him from the blinding sun.

5

When night came the men went to the mosque for the evening prayer and then gathered around Salem Ahmad. No one went to sea.

"We must beat the drum by the shore. Maybe that thing'll get scared and flee," said Zahed.

"I'm scared. I'm scared of the sound of drums," Salem moaned.

"Don't worry. Nothing is the matter with you. You've been frightened. That's all," said Zahed.

"The sea is so loud tonight, I don't think any one will hear the drums," said Saleh.

"We'll get around that somehow . I want someone to fetch my timbal and drums," said Zahed.

"Mohammad Ahmad Ali, go fetch Zahed's timbal and drums," Zakariya said.

"All by myself?" said Mohammad Ahmad Ali, getting up.

"Yes, go by yourself, but don't fall asleep in the shack," said Saleh.

"I'm scared. I'm worried," said Mohammad Ahmad Ali.

"All right, I'll go with you. Stop complaining," said Abd al-Javad.

Mohammad Ahmad Ali and Abd al-Javad headed toward the Ayyub reservoir.

"I don't think Salem Ahmad is going to make it. When he was lying behind the coffin he threw up several times," Mohammad Ahmad Ali said.

"I hope to God Zahed will be able to help him," Abd al-Javad said.

"I hope so too."

"An amulet wouldn't hurt, either."

"I wouldn't think so. Zahed said amulets won't work. We've got to beat the drum."

They circled the rear of the Ayyub reservoir now in deep shadow. Avoiding the black patch, they hurried to Zahed's shack. It had become stormy and the high pounding seas filled the dark horizon.

"Go inside and get the drums," urged Abd al-Javad.

"Why don't you go in yourself?"

"I don't like to go into the wild man's shack this time of night."

"I'm only afraid of the shadows."

"I'll stand watch here."

Mohammad Ahmad Ali pushed the curtain aside and went in. A few moments later a drum boomed and Mohammad Ahmad Ali appeared with a large drum. Abd al-Javad took the drum, and Mohammad Ahmad Ali went back and returned with another drum and timbal. He laid them on the ground and went back inside, returning with several drumsticks. He slung the drum over his shoulder and tucked the timbal under his arm. Abd al-Javad picked up the large drum and they began walking side by side. Rounding the dark spot again, they reached the reservoir but suddenly heard a strange sound, the sound of an invisible object being inflated in the water. Mohammad Ahmad Ali and Abd al-Javad, their feet flying, retreated to the village, to find the mosque deserted.

"Where have they all gone?" cried Mohammad Ahmad Ali.

Then, seeing a dim light near the shore, they hurried toward it. There, the men had gathered on the sandy shore around an overturned rowboat. Zakariya was standing on top of it, a lantern in his hand. Zahed was holding a bowl of water to Salem Ahmad's lips. Abd al-Javad and Mohammad Ahmad Ali came up and put the drums on the ground and waited.

Zahed chanced to look back and saw them.

"O God! O Mohammad! Now we must beat the drums until morning," he exclaimed.

The sea had grown more clamorous; the wind raged as the drums moaned.

6

When the sun rose, the men put the drums aside and sat on the ground, exhausted. The sea had quieted down and was changing color. Suddenly Salem Ahmad screamed out, indicating his horror at what he saw in the distance, near his house. The men then looked that way, to discover the parlor door that was now ajar and a thin black man standing just outside, supported on two crutches. His head was wrapped in a red headcloth, and his galabiya reached the ground.

The men rose and backed away, horrified. The Black watched them without moving.

"In the name of God, faith and religion, leave this village alone!" Zahed shouted.

All were silent. The Black did not move. Zahed took one step toward him. The men followed suit.

"Do you hear me?" Zahed screamed.

The Black did not answer.

"Do you hear me or not?" Zahed shouted again.

"Maybe he doesn't understand what you say," Saleh Kamzari said.

"Why did you come here? Where did you come from?" Zahed hollered.

"You're not loud enough, Zahed. Let Zakariya talk to him," suggested Saleh.

Zakariya stepped closer to the Black and boomed out, "Why did you come here? Where do you come from? What do you want?"

The Black said nothing.

"Do you hear me? Do you?" Zakariya shouted.

"Tell him we aren't going to hurt him. Tell him to pick up and leave," said Zahed.

"Leave this place," Zakariya shouted angrily.

"Come! Leave this place! Go away!" Saleh Kamzari also shouted.

"Go away! Get out of here!" the men shouted together.

The Black hobbled closer on his crutches. The men backed away.

"Say something. Can't you talk?" Zakariya shouted.

They heard a low sound, almost like a laughter.

"What did he say?" asked Mohammad Ahmad Ali.

"What did you say? Speak louder," Zakariya screamed.

The Black stepped closer. Salem Ahmad groaned behind the men. The men took one step toward the Black and Zakariya shouted.

"What do you want?"

"Help me!" the Black said.

"What did he say?" Zahed asked.

"He said, 'help me,'" said Zakariya.

"Help you? May God damn you!" muttered Saleh.

"Help him with what?" Abd al-Javad asked Zahed.

Zahed turned to the men.

"Don't pay him any attention. Don't listen to him. It's a trick," he said.

The Black came closer. The men stepped back.

"Stop where you are!" Zakariya shouted.

The Black raised one hand and pleaded.

"Help! Help!"

"What kind of help?" Zakariya said.

"O Prophet of God! He keeps coming closer," said Mohammad Ahmad Ali.

"I can't make him out. I can't tell what he wants to do. Be careful. He wants to trick us," said Zahed, backing away.

"What do you want? If you have anything to say, say it. Stop coming closer," Zakariya said.

"I want bread," the Black said.

"He's lying. He doesn't want bread. He wants to come closer until we're possessed," said Zahed.

"What else do you want?" Zakariya shouted.

"Why are you asking him these questions?" Saleh said.

"I want to know what he wants here," said Zakariya.

"That's good. Ask him. Ask him what he wants here," said Zahed.

"Do you want anything other than bread?" Zakariya shouted.

"I want bread. I want fish. Fish, too," said the Black.

"What else? What else do you want to eat?" Zakariya said.

"Dates. I like dates, too," said the Black.

"How cocky!" said Mohammad Ahmad Ali.

"God damn him. I know what he wants. It's not bread and dates. It's something else he's after," said Zahed.

"How about cheese? Don't you want cheese?" said Zakariya.

"I want cheese, too," said the Black.

"What about rice? Don't you like rice?" said Zakariya.

"I do. I like rice a lot," said the Black.

"God damn you!" said Zahed, then turned to the men. "I know what he wants. Not rice. He wants something else."

"There is no God but Allah and Mohammad is his Messenger," Mohammad Hajji Mostafa recited the creed to ward off evil.

"What are we to do now?" Kadkhoda turned to Zahed.

"Ask him what he's going to do? Is he leaving or not?" said Zahed to Zakariya.

The black man hobbled slowly closer; the men again backed away, keeping an eye on one another.

"What are you going to do? Are you leaving this place or aren't you?" Zakariya shouted.

"No, I don't want to leave this place," said the Black.

Salem's name was called from the sea.

"What did he say?" Zahed asked.

"He isn't planning to leave," said Mohammad Hajji Mostafa.

They turned and looked at Zahed.

"If he doesn't leave, Salem is done for. We're all done for," Zahed said.

"You mean we'll all be possessed?" asked Mohammad Ahmad Ali.

"Of course," said Zahed.

"Can't we drive him away somehow?" said Kadkhoda.

"That's what we should do," said Zahed.

"Let's catch him and throw him into the sea," said Mohammad Hajji Mostafa.

"I don't think we could do that," said Zakariya.

"He's getting closer! Think of something!" said Mohammad Ahmad Ali.

"Will it be a sin if we kill him?" said Zakariya.

"It won't be, if he's a *mazarrati*," said Zahed.

"Of course he's a *mazarrati*," Mohammad Hajji Mostafa said.

"If he weren't, Salem wouldn't be possessed now," said Abd al-Javad.

"Even if we kill him, he'll turn up somewhere else," said Zahed. "His kind won't stop until the end of time."

"He keeps coming closer. Look at him! Look at him!" said Zakariya.

The black man was very close. His face was quite flat, as if his nose and lips had been gnawed away.

Zahed bent down and picked up a rock.

"I take leave from God and the Prophet of God," he cried, hurling the rock at the black man.

The Black, intimidated, backed away.

"He's moving off! Don't let him get away!" Zakariya shouted at the men.

"I'm hungry, I'm hungry," the black man pleaded.

The men each picked up a rock and hurled it at the black man.

"I want bread. I want dates. I want cheese!" the Black cried.

"It's not bread he wants. It's not dates and cheese he wants. I know what he's after," said Zahed.

"I'm hungry," the Black moaned.

"Don't let him get away," Zahed repeated.

Saleh hurled a big rock at the Black, hitting his wooden leg. The Black rolled to the ground.

"Taking leave from God! Don't let him get away," Zahed cried.

Each man picked a rock and together they charged at the Black.

7

Three days and nights passed and Salem Ahmad took a turn for the worse. He would run around the houses and scream and moan. He couldn't eat, and the silhouette of the date palms terrified him.

Zahed had told the men not to go out to sea and they had followed his advice. The rowboats remained idle on the shore. The villagers had beaten the drum and used amulets, but to no avail. Peace had left their lives. At night, an evil force churned the sea and terrified the villagers.

On the third day the men tied up Salem Ahmad with a rope and took him to the mosque's entrance.

"Poor Salem Ahmad, I don't think he's going to make it," Zahed said.

"Isn't there something you could do for him?" said Mohammad Hajji Mostafa.

"I can't do anything. Only God can cure him," said Zahed.

Salem roared and struggled, the rope entangling his arms and legs.

"Maybe it would help if we took Salem to him," said Zahed to the villagers.

"Take Salem to him? What for?" Mohammad Ahmad Ali objected.

"Hey, Zahed, if you want to do poor Salem in, let me tell you right away you can count me out," said Abd al-Javad.

"We've got to take Salem to him and get the cure," said Zahed.

"Not a bad idea. Maybe he'll cure Salem," said Saleh.

The men began to walk toward the mound of rocks,* dragging Salem Ahmad along. The closer they got, the louder Salem Ahmad moaned. At the mound, Zakariya tied the loose end of the rope to the anchor of an old boat. Then they all walked away from Salem Ahmad.

"Someone should go and fetch him some food," said Zahed.

Something evil prowled the air and the sea grew darker.

"Go to my house and fetch a jug of water and some dates," Zakariya said to Mohammad Ahmad Ali.

Mohammad Ahmad Ali hurried toward the village and the men followed slowly. They had not taken more than a few steps when Salem Ahmad's moaning stopped abruptly. They looked back. He was sitting on the mound, gazing at the sea.

"What happened?" said Mohammad Hajji Mostafa.

"He's getting better. May it please God, he'll be all right," said Zahed joyfully.

Salem sat motionless, facing the sea. The sea clamored. Far away, a kind voice was calling Salem's name.

---

*The mound piled over the black man, whom they had stoned.

SECOND STORY

Zakariya and Mohammad Ahmad Ali had just returned from the sea and were pulling the boat ashore when an old pickup truck turned the corner noiselessly and emerged from behind the ruins. It stopped at the slope of the shore. The driver, a bearded man, thrust his head out of the window, looking first at the sea and then at the two men. The two passengers in the front seat were inert and lumpish, like the driver. All three were wearing dark glasses.

"God have mercy on us! Who on earth are these?" Mohammad Ahmad Ali whispered.

"Never mind. Don't look at them. Let them be," said Zakariya.

"They can't be from around here. They've got to be strangers. I wonder what they are doing here."

"Well, they're here now. They can come here if they want to. You can't tell them not to, can you?"

"They're glued there, watching us."

"You're still afraid of everything. If you're really scared, just go back to sea."

"Could they be Arabs?"

"Arabs? What if they were? Since when have you been afraid of Arabs?"

"I'm not afraid, Zakariya; I'm not afraid of Arabs. I was just asking."

"Well, don't. You talk a lot of nonsense when you're scared."

"I hope they leave. I don't want to worry about them," Mohammad Ahmad Ali complained, grabbing the prow and pulling the boat farther ashore.

The driver honked his horn. Zakariya and Mohammad Ahmad Ali let go of the boat and looked at the strangers. A man, about forty and wearing an army cap, thrust his head out through the canvas back of the van and beckoned them to approach.

"Don't you go over there, Zakariya!" Mohammad Ahmad Ali warned.

"Why shouldn't I? I'm not afraid of everything the way you are."

"I'm not afraid of everything. Only of strangers."

"I'm not even afraid of strangers." Zakariya wrapped his cloth around his head and stepped towards the pickup.

The heavily bearded man in the military cap called out, "Hello!"

"Hello! Hello, welcome!" said Zakariya.

"How many houses are there in this village?"

"A lot."

"What about date palms? Any palm groves?"

"Sure!"

"What kind of work do the people do?"

"They mostly fish."

"A good place isn't it?"

"It's good for us. I don't know about others."

The man laughed.

"It's good for others too," he said. "God blesses any place where there's man, so this must be a good spot."

He lifted his legs out of the van and jumped down. He was short, with a big, square trunk, a round head, enormous arms and hands, but legs no bigger than a child's. An old leather bag hung around his neck by a piece of rope. Two pens hung from his shirt pocket. Zakariya watched him, wondering how a man of forty could be so short.

The man waved to the driver. The two men in the front seat nodded. The driver adjusted his glasses and drove off. Zakariya, followed by the newcomer, returned to Mohammad Ahmad Ali, who had stayed with the boat. The newcomer greeted him.

"Hurry up! Let's go to the village. We have a guest," Zakariya said to Mohammad Ahmad Ali.

The newcomer sat next to Mohammad Ahmad Ali's full basket of fish, and took a cigarette out of his bag. Zakariya and Mohammad Ahmad Ali dragged the boat further up the beach. The newcomer lit his cigarette.

"Don't you have those things they put under boats to roll them out more easily?" he asked Mohammad Ahmad Ali.

"Yes we do, for big boats. We can manage this one without," said Mohammad Ahmad Ali.

Zakariya lifted the anchor and dropped it onto the sand. The anchor rope shook the boat. Mohammad Ahmad Ali pushed a half-burned log under the indented underside of the prow and waited. The newcomer rose and the three men started for the village, the stranger waddling a few steps ahead of the other two.

"Who is he looking for?" Mohammad Ahmad Ali whispered to Zakariya.

"I don't know. Somebody, I guess."

"What is he looking for? What does he want?"

"I don't know what he wants."

"Maybe he is here to conscript men."

"No, he doesn't have a gun."

"He's probably got something in his bag."

"Like what?"

"Something he could scare us with."

"You're imagining things again."

"I'm not. Don't you see his cap?"

Zakariya laughed, shaking his head.

"Only gendarmes come to conscript men. He isn't a gendarme. Maybe he's here to give us birth certificates,"* he said.

"I don't know. What should we do if he wants to give us birth certificates, Zakariya?"

"Nothing. Let him write out as many certificates as he wants."

"I for one don't want any. If he tries to force me to get one, I'll run away."

"Why run away?"

"I don't want them to write my name in their book."

"Are you two tired, or are you lagging behind so you can chat?" the newcomer said, looking over his shoulder.

"Working at sea tires one out," said Zakariya.

"It's almost time for evening prayer. We were wondering whether we should go straight to the mosque," said Mohammad Ahmad Ali.

They passed through two rows of houses and stopped before the mosque's apron. The newcomer looked back at the sea below them and smiled. Mohammad Ahmad Ali also looked back at the sea. Zakariya nudged Mohammad Ahmad Ali, who shrank with fear. The village men were sitting under the mosque's portico, waiting for the sun to go down. Mohammad Hajji Mostafa had done his ablution and was sitting on the coffin with his sleeves rolled up, ready to recite the *izan*.** When they saw the three men, they rose. The newcomer greeted them.

"Welcome. How are you?" said Mohammad Hajji Mostafa.

"What brings you here?" said Kadkhoda, stepping closer.

"I had a sudden urge to come to this village. I hear water is plenty here.

* Suspicious of all government agencies and officials, the inhabitants of remote Persian Gulf areas prefer not to get birth certificates (or identity cards, *sejel*), since certificates would enable the government to keep track of them. See Sa'edi's *Ahl-i Hava*, p. 17.
** The call to the prayer.

Is that true?" the newcomer said.

"It's enough for us to survive. We've got three reservoirs and a well," said Kadkhoda.

"What about a mullah? Have you got a mullah?" said the newcomer.

"What on earth for? We don't send letters, and we don't need amulets and charms, praised be the Lord!" said Mohammad Ahmad Ali.

"I'm glad you don't have a mullah, because I'm a mullah and I can write. If any of you want to send a letter or need an amulet, you can come to me, for I intend to stay here for a while," said the newcomer.

"We haven't got a mullah, but we have Zahed, who's a black man. He's a good man, has certain skills. He plays the drum and recites prayers, but he doesn't know how to write," said Kadkhoda.

"There are other things I can do. I can undo evil spells. I have certain gifts. I have other powers, and I have money too," said the newcomer.

"Poor Zahed isn't like that. He's indigent. He lives in a shack behind the reservoir," said Mohammad Hajji Mostafa.

"Please ,it down. Take a rest," said Kadkhoda to the newcomer.

The r)u lah removed his bag from around his neck and sat at the head of the sɪɪaɔ mat in the place of honor.

"When does the sun set here?" he asked.

Zakariya turned, looking at the sky and the sea.

"Whenever it wants to. It's kind of strange," Mohammad Ahmad Ali said to the mullah.

2

After the evening prayer the village men went to Kadkhoda's house. Someone fetched a lamp from Mohammad Hajji Mostafa's place. The mullah entered followed by Kadkhoda and the rest, looked around him, then went to the head of the room, in the place of honor, and sat down, leaning against the cushions and gathering his legs under him. Kadkhoda's son brought water. The mullah washed his hands in the basin, then removing his cap placed it on the pillow. He moved his bag and put it beside him. Zakariya and Mohammad Ahmad Ali felt embarrassed because they had not the means to put up the guest and he was staying with Kadkhoda. Kadkhoda fetched the dinner cloth and spread it on the floor, in front of the mullah; then he and the men left the room. The mullah glanced at the empty dinner cloth, then looked out of the room. Darkness hung at the door like a thick curtain. Kadkhoda's son emerged with a big tray. The smell of spices and raw onions filled the room. The mullah, shifting his position, took the tray and put it down before himself. Kadkhoda's son left. The village men were sitting outside in the dark, just beyond the porch.

"Did you take him water?" Kadkhoda asked.

"I did," his son replied.

"Well, go wait at the door. When he finishes eating, call us so we can go in and chat," said Kadkhoda.

Kadkhoda's son returned to the room and stood at the door. The mullah was eating hurriedly, swallowing without chewing, downing every mouthful with a gulp of water. He finished the food, then washed his hands in the basin. Raising his head, he noticed Kadkhoda's son at the door and smiled.

"Would you like anything else?" Kadkhoda's son asked.

"No, just make my bed so I can sleep," said the mullah.

"My father wanted to come in and chat for a while."

"It's too late. Too late to sit around and chat."

Kadkhoda's son spread the bedding on the floor. The mullah lay down and fell asleep instantly. Kadkhoda's son took the lamp and returned to the men outside.

"Why did you take out the lamp?" asked Zakariya.

"He said he didn't want to chat. He wanted to go to sleep, and he did," said Kadkhoda's son.

3

At dawn, when Kadkhoda returned from the morning prayer at the mosque, he looked into the room to call the mullah but found it empty. The bedding still lay in the middle of the room.

"The mullah has gone," Kadkhoda said to his son.

"Where?" His son looked into the room.

"I don't know. Maybe he's left the village."

"He can't leave the village. Where could he go if he left?"

"Well, he isn't here."

"Maybe he's gone out to say his prayer."

"We just came from the mosque. He wasn't there."

"Maybe he wanted to say his prayer by the sea."

Kadkhoda surveyed the seashore behind him, but saw no one. On the horizon a few small boats floated on the water like matchboxes.

"He's not there, either," said Kadkhoda.

"Don't worry. He won't go anywhere. His things are all here."

"I'm not worried. No big deal even if he's left. I just want to know whether to make tea."

"We'd better make some. If he doesn't drink it we will."

"Except that guests like their tea mild and I like mine strong."

"Well, compromise and make it mild today."

"There he is! He's coming!" Kadkhoda exclaimed.

The mullah appeared in the alley, waddling, his long arms and big hands swinging back and forth.

"Good morning, Kadkhoda. You're well, I hope," he said when he got nearer.

"Good morning. Thank you. How are you yourself? Where were you?"

"I went to the outskirts of the village to say my prayer. Then I went to the palm grove, saw the reservoir, walked around in the village, and came back," said the mullah.

"I hope you liked it."

"I liked it all right. I saw the date palms. Knock on wood, you've got lots of *shekari** and *mosalla*."

"Yes, and *zamardun* too."

"*Zamardun* too? How nice. I didn't notice any, though. What other kinds have you got?"

"We also have *kabkab*."

"Really? You've got *kabkab* too? I like *kabkab* dates."

"May you eat them in good health."

"What else do you have, other than *kabkab* and *zamardun*?"

"We've got *shekari*, and we've got *mosalla*."

"In Mohammad Hajji Mostafa's grove there are about fifty *qantars*," said Kadkhoda's son.

"Fifty *qantars*! Knock on wood! Knock on wood! Fifty *qantars*! How nice," said the mullah.

"Yes, there are fifty *qantars* in Mohammad Hajji Mostafa's grove," Kadkhoda confirmed.

"What about your grove? I mean good varieties?" said the mullah.

---

* The italicized words in this and the following page are names for different types of dates grown in the South of Iran.

"In our grove we've got *shekari, mosalla,* and four *kabkabs,*" said Kadkhoda.

"What about *zamardun?* Have you got any?" asked the mullah.

"Yes, that too," said Kadkhoda's son.

"Tell me, do you have any *pangderaz* in this village? You know what ꞁ talking about?" said the mullah.

"Yes, you might well ask. *Pangderaz* is excellent," said Kadkhoda.

"We've got some on the other side of the Ayyub reservoir, in a small grove. It doesn't belong to anybody. It's Zahed's, so to speak. The same black man who plays the drum," said Kadkhoda's son.

"And?" said the mullah.

"Once I saw a few *pangderaz* palms there. Zahed doesn't know what they are. Other people pick the dates," said Kadkhoda's son.

"Excellent! Excellent!" said the mullah.

"May your honor increase! May God grant you a long life," said Kadkhoda.

"You know, Kadkhoda, I love to eat them," said the mullah.

"Eat what?" asked Kadkhoda's son.

"What I mentioned—*zamardun, kabkab, dagal,* and *shekari* dates, especially yellow *shekari,*" said the mullah.

"Good, eat them. Eat them all," said Kadkhoda.

"When I eat *zamardun* my back and arms and legs stop aching," said the mullah.

"Sure, it cures everything," said Kadkhoda.

"*Kabkab* makes me feel exhilarated. I like it because it's mild," said the mullah.

"I didn't know about that," said Kadkhoda.

"*Kabkab* is even more beneficial if you eat it after fried eggs. It's got all kinds of virtues," said the mullah.

"I didn't know these things. I guess it is as you say," said Kadkhoda.

"Yes, Sir, each of God's blessings has a virtue all its own. One cures headache, another backache, a third is good for a married man. If you eat *shekari* in the morning and *mosalla* in the evening you'll feel more exhilarated than you ever thought possible," said the mullah.

"Absolutely! If you can find that kind of date and eat it! Of course you'll feel exhilarated. But, Mullah, we don't have that much, not enough so you could eat that kind every day. Only Mohammad Hajji Mostafa is well off around here, but even his grove isn't that big. Besides, he's got a big family and also helps out the blacks. He's a God-fearing man," said Kadkhoda.

"You've got a point. But I've read in books that each variety of date

palm was created for a reason. Date palms are just like people. You se
how people are different? Date palms are just the same. God does nothing
without a reason," said the mullah.

"Excellent, Mullah! You're a learned man," said Kadkhoda.

"I'll fetch some tea. Would you prefer mild or strong tea?" said
Kadkhoda's son.

"Makes no difference," said the mullah.

"Let's have black tea, then," said Kadkhoda's son and went toward the
house.

"Sit down, Mullah. You'll get tired if you don't," invited Kadkhoda.

Kadkhoda sat down. The mullah sat down too, but sitting down he was
only a span shorter than he was, standing up.

"You know, Kadkhoda, a place which doesn't have good women, good
water, and good dates isn't fit for living. How old do you think I am? I am
much older than you, and see, you can't find a gray hair on my head. But
try and find a black one in yours! You know why? Because I don't believe
in roughing it. Every place I go I pick a good woman, and I eat well. By the
way, Kadkhoda, that big door in the first alley, whose house is that?"

"Which door?"

"The large studded door above which hangs a pair of antlers."

"O that! That's Zakariya's house. Why?"

"When I was walking by the reservoir I saw a tall, plump woman
fetching water. On the way back, I wasn't paying much attention, but I saw
her enter that house. Is she married?"

"Ah she! She's Zakariya's sister and she isn't married. That is, she was
married, but her husband divorced her when he went to the Island."

"I could tell she wasn't married," the mullah laughed. "I could tell by
the way she walked. You see what a good place I've come to, Kadkhoda! I
want you to go to Zakariya in an hour or so and ask him whether his sister
wants to get married. Then tell him there is a servant of God who's a
mullah, who can write, has money, and is looking for a wife. If he says yes,
tell him it's his lucky day, and seal the bargain."

"I'll go, but we'll have to wait until the sun rises and Zakariya comes
back from the sea."

"Do you think he'll agree?"

"Of course. There's no two ways about it."

"Excellent, Kadkhoda. You're a very sensible man. I've been married
many times. I know what sort of woman is good and what sort is bad.
Which will suit me, and which won't. Some make you happy, some
don't. Some cheer you up, some make you miserable. But I've read in

books that womankind is all good. She's the cure to a bachelor's every problem. When you're down, she's the only answer. Yes, God's doings aren't without reason."

"Excellent, Mullah. The problem is you need money to marry. Everybody knows what the benefits are!"

"Excellent, Kadkhoda. But I always have money. Now go and get this woman for me."

Kadkhoda's son appeared with a bathroom pitcher so the guest could wash up. The mullah squatted, and Kadkhoda's son poured the water into his hands. The mullah splashed his face. With the second handful he filled his mouth and rinsed his teeth and gums. After spitting the water out he kept his mouth open—a few seconds later, a swarm of tiny flies flew out from the depth of his throat.

4

Kadkhoda went to Zakariya's house and returned to find the mullah sitting at the window, his legs gathered under his heavy trunk.

"What happened?" he asked.

"Zakariya wasn't home. He's at sea, fishing; hasn't come back yet."

"When will he be back?"

Kadkhoda glanced at the sea.

"He's with Mohammad Ahmad Ali. It's time they came back," he said. "Let's go look for them by the sea."

At the sea shore the two men sat on an overturned boat and waited. Fishing boats were scattered over the sea, as motionless as dead fish embedded in ice.

"When do you think they'll get here?" asked the mullah.

"When they feel like it. Zakariya always gets back before the rest," said Kadkhoda.

"Isn't that the two of them walking this way?"

Kadkhoda shaded his eyes with his hand.

"Yes, there they are," he said. "Zakariya! Hey, Zakariya!" he called out.

"Hey! Hey!" Mohammad Ahmad Ali responded.

"Zakariya! Zakariya!" Kadkhoda shouted again.

Mohammad Ahmad Ali and Zakariya reached Kadkhoda and the mullah and the men exchanged greetings.

"How was the sea? Good, I hope," said Kadkhoda.

"Good, God bless her. If she isn't kind one day, she makes up for it the next, Kadkhoda," said Zakariya.

"Praised be the Lord! Now sit down for a minute. The mullah and I have some business to discuss with you. He wants to marry your sister. He says he's got money and he'll give you something for her. One less mouth to feed, so what do you say? Will you give him your sister?"

Zakariya sat down, scrutinizing the mullah's short legs and enormous arms.

"Pardon my mentioning this, Kadkhoda, but my wife is expecting—she won't be long now. My sister has been fetching us water from the reservoir. If I marry her off, we won't have anybody to fetch us water," he said.

"He's right, Mullah. If he gives you his sister, there won't be anyone to fetch them water," Kadkhoda said to the mullah.

"That isn't a problem. I'll tell her to carry water to your house twice a day," the mullah said.

"There's something else, too. My sister's former husband has gone to the Island. He promised to marry her again when he comes back at the end of the summer. I've promised her to him. What am I to do about that?" said Zakariya.

The mullah lit a cigarette.

"Come now! It's a long time before the end of summer. Besides, if he shows up, just tell him you found a good man and gave her to him. It's simple. A bird in the hand is worth two in the bush," he said.

"There are other things. For one thing, you don't have a place of your own. Besides . . . ," said Zakariya.

"I'll think of something," the mullah interrupted. "I'll take one of those empty houses in the village and fix it up, or I'll build one. If that doesn't work out, I'll build a hut, since summer is approaching, until it gets cooler."

"Besides," Zakariya continued, "my sister is the best woman around here. I'm not saying that because she's my sister; everybody knows she's the best. The expenses of such a woman are high. Do you think you can afford such a wife?"

"I'll take care of her expenses, don't worry. I'll pay, be it high or low. Is there anything else?" said the mullah.

Zakariya considered the proposal, then looked the mullah over from head to toe.

"Well, to tell the truth . . . ," he hesitated.

"What, you have reservations? If you don't want to give her to me, say so. Don't be afraid," the mullah said.

"To tell you the truth, I don't even know who you are."

"Me? You know who I am. I can write, I'm a mullah, and I've money."

"I know all that. You can write, you write letters, but . . ."

"There's no but. I'm a Moslem. You believe that, don't you? I travel around. I'm a fair person; I'm not looking just for an extra mouth to feed. I believe in the law of the Prophet of God and I want to take a wife."

Kadkhoda and Mohammad Ahmad Ali recited the *salavat.**

"It makes no difference to me," the mullah continued. "Your sister or somebody else's sister, it's all the same to me—except that I've heard your sister is better. If you like the idea of having one less mouth to feed, say yes."

"He's got a point, Zakariya. You'll have one less mouth to feed," said Kadkhoda.

Zakariya was hesitant. He looked at Mohammad Ahmad Ali.

"I guess Kadkhoda is right. It's the law of the Prophet, greetings to him, and you can't do anything about it," said Mohammad Ahmad Ali.

Zakariya thought the matter over.

"Congratulations! Come to my house at noon; there'll be a piece of fish and a handful of dates to eat," he said to the mullah.

"Come, Mullah," said Mohammad Ahmad Ali. "I'll go to Zakariya's too. He told me if the catch was good I could go to his house and eat at his dinner cloth. Thank God, the catch was good. God bless her, both yesterday and today the sea was very kind."

The men turned and looked lovingly at the smooth, calm sea.

5

When they finished lunch, Zakariya's sister entered the room and sat in a dark corner. The marriage formula had been recited before lunch. Mohammad Ahmad Ali had left after eating his fish and dates. The mullah was sitting in the place of honor. With his short legs gathered beneath his squat trunk, he looked as if he were taller than Zakariya. He had removed his cap and placed his bag beside him. Zakariya's sister sat facing the wall, refusing to look anywhere else. The mullah rubbed his stomach.

"I read somewhere in a book that nothing is as necessary and

---

* The benediction, meaning, "O God bless Mohammad and his descendants."

indispensable as food," he said.

"If it was written in a book, it must be true," said Zakariya.

"Yes, the book said the person who eats well, feels well; his head and joints don't ache; his pains go away."

"It's probably as you say."

"Yes the lunch quite agreed with my constitution. I feel good, happy, light—not bloated."

"Praise the Lord!"

"But there's something else I'm in the habit of doing. I don't sleep after good food, or after anything good for that matter. If I eat bad food I sleep, which has several benefits. First, you forget the taste of the food. Second, the stomach does its job better and digests the food quicker. Third, sleep absorbs the food's venom. But I don't sleep after good food. First, so I won't forget its taste. Second, so it isn't digested too fast. Third, because good food has no venom so no sleep is needed. Good food, or anything good, gives you energy; you get up and go. You understand? You feel good. I read all this in a book."

"I don't know what to say. Fishing is all I know about. Zahed knows a few things, but not the sort of things you're talking about."

"No, you've got to have books. Without books nothing is of any use."

"Right. You, for instance, need books; and I, I need a boat and oars and fish."

"Yes, Zakariya, everybody needs some particular thing. That was a wise statement you made."

"Sure! For example, if you don't have a home, what can you do? Sleep in the desert or out in the sea?"

"You're right. Can't I use one of these empty houses?"

"You can. Anyone you want, but they're all in ruins."

"Don't worry. I'll pay and fix one up."

"When?"

"This afternoon. And I'll get together floor mats, pots and pans, whatever we need."

"From where?"

"I'll buy them."

"We don't have a bazaar here."

"No problem. This evening I'll announce in the mosque that anyone with pots and pans or floor mats and mattresses to sell, can bring them to me."

"I wish you success."

"Yes, Zakariya, the Prophet's law says when you marry a woman, you must think about her comfort. After all, she is a Moslem too, and a servant of God."

Zakariya's sister looked over her shoulder at her brother and then at the mullah, who lowered his head, not wanting to look at her in her brother's presence.

6

In the evening Zakariya accompanied the mullah to the mosque. The house was ready. Zakariya and Mohammad Ahmad Ali had helped the mullah with the repairs and had been paid right away. Saleh was reciting the *izan* from the platform next to the coffin. His voice was heard all through the village. The mullah, his cap in his hand and his bag slung over his shoulder, strode toward the mosque with his short legs. There was no lamp in the mosque, but the moon shone through an opening in the ceiling, lighting the center of the floor, where Mohammad Ahmad Ali and Abd al-Javad were sitting. A hole in the *mehrab** revealed the pale moonlight which the men gazed upon during their prayer. When the prayer was over, the mullah went to the *mehrab* and stood with his back to the light.

"Let's see what he has to say," said Saleh.

"Folks, I need a couple of pots, a few bowls, a pair of sandals, a lamp, a few floor mats, two mattresses, and a few blankets. I'll pay cash. If you have any of these things bring them over," said the mullah.

"Who's this stranger?" asked Zahed.

"It's the mullah. He's married Zakariya's sister and wants to set up house," said Kadkhoda. "Come everybody! Sell what you have to the mullah."

"How can we sell what we have? What will we do then?" Saleh said.

"I mean what you have no use for, understand? Whatever is extra and you don't want," said Kadkhoda.

"I see, what we don't need. I've got two swords I want to sell," said Abd al-Javad.

"I don't want swords; I don't need swords," said the mullah.

"Wouldn't you want to hang them on the wall?" said Abd al-Javad.

---

* A decorative panel designating the *kiblah*, the point toward which Moslems turn to pray.

"He doesn't want swords, Abd al-Javad. He wants things that he can use around the house," said Kadkhoda.

"I didn't say he had to buy them. That's all I have. If he wants them he can have them; if not, I'll keep them," said Abd al-Javad.

"God bless you Abd al-Javad," Kadkhoda said.

"May your honor increase," Abd al-Javad responded.

"Kadkhoda, I've nothing to sell. What shall I do?" said Mohammad Ahmad Ali.

"Nothing. If you haven't got anything, what have you got to sell?" said Saleh Kamzari.

"I've got a big chest without a lid. I'll sell it if you want it," said Kadkhoda's son.

"If you want drums or bamboo sticks I can sell you some," said Zahed.

"It's dark now. He can't tell what he's getting in the dark. Tomorrow morning, when you come back from the sea, bring whatever you have to my house. The mullah will buy the things he needs," said Kadkhoda.

"Excellent! Excellent!" said the mullah.

The men left the mosque. The sea was clamorous and the shadow of the moon pressed heavily over the water. The mullah, followed by Zakariya, set out toward the first alley.

"The north wind has started," said Mohammad Ahmad Ali cheerfully.

The men stopped, gratefully filling their lungs with the cool evening breeze.

7

When the mullah and Zakariya reached Kadkhoda's house they found a large crowd in front of the house, the men near the door and the women behind them. In the middle of the small square there was a heap of household items. There were broken dishes, lamps, pots and pans, stools, old blankets, floor mats, terra-cotta bowls, antique swords, walking sticks, drums, hand mills, daggers, coffee-makers of all sizes, buckets, pitchers, troughs, narrow-waisted Arabic tea-glasses, old flour bags, bathroom pitchers, oars and a few chairs.

When the mullah appeared, the women huddled closer together. He was lifting his legs high, taking the longest steps he could. Reaching the crowd, he removed his shoulder bag and sat on Kadkhoda's porch.

Kadkhoda walked out of the crowd and sat beside him.

"Well, Mullah, this is what we have," said Mohammad Hajji Mostafa, who was squatting on the ground.

The mullah stared at the disorderly pile of household articles.

"You brought all of this for me?" he asked.

"Of course we brought it all for you. We hope you'll like and buy it all," said Mohammad Hajji Mostafa.

"I don't need all that. Just a couple of pots, a few floor mats, the things I mentioned at the mosque last night," said the mullah.

He passed through the crowd and picked up a small pot.

"Who does this belong to?" he asked.

"It belongs to an old woman," said Saleh, pointing at the crowd of women.

"What am I supposed to do with this? Come, take a look, Zakariya. It's full of holes! What could you cook in this? Rice? Fish? Or cattle food. Take it back, Mother. I don't have any use for it," the mullah said.

"For God's sake take it and give me a little something for it. I am destitute," a woman said in the crowd.

"Take it for what? If no one can use it how do you expect me to? Come, Zakariya, tell them I always go after good things and pick the best," said the mullah. He lifted a broken lamp stand. "Whatever is this?"

"It's a lamp stand. It used to be a lamp, before it fell and broke. This is what's left of it," said Saleh.

"So what do you suggest I do with it?" asked the mullah.

"Put it on the mantle, in front of the window. It's fine as it is. You may find an oil-can some day, which you can stick to the stand and make yourself a brand new lamp," said Saleh.

"Thanks a lot," said the mullah. "I want a lamp, not a lamp stand."

"Well, if you don't want it buy these ropes. If you ever buy a canoe or a skiff, or even a rowboat, you can tie it with this rope in the sand so the wind won't drive it away," said Saleh.

"Hang it! You don't seem to understand!" exclaimed the mullah.

"We do. We've got a lot of things you could use. Don't you want a terra-cotta jug so you can drink cool water? Don't you want swords to hang on your wall?" said Saleh.

"No, I don't. I want things I can use. Every village I go to I get myself good things and a good wife. Now that I'm here, I want good things," said the mullah.

"But we want the good stuff ourselves," said Saleh.

"What for? I've got money. I'll give you money for them," said the mullah.

"You expect us to sell you the good stuff?" said Saleh.

"Look at it this way, Saleh. Decide which is better, which you like better, money or pots, money or mattresses," said Kadkhoda.

"Probably money is better," mumbled Mohammad Ahmad Ali, who was dozing off.

"This won't work," said the mullah. "I'm going to send Zakariya to search every house and buy the things he likes."

"Fine," said Kadkhoda.

The villagers rose, picked their household articles and started for their homes.

8

It was a clamorous night, the sea roaring, the wind riotous. Zahed and Mohammad Ahmad Ali sat waiting by the graveyard with two big drums. Shadows filled all the alleys, and footsteps echoed everywhere in the village.

"The mullah has forbidden them to beat the drum, but she insists she won't get married without drums," said Zahed.

"She's right, isn't she, Zahed?" responded Mohammad Ahmad Ali.

"Of course she's right. Too bad we're poor and can't afford to marry."

"If I were to get married, I'd beat the drums for seven days, wouldn't I, Zahed? Too bad there's no chance of that," Mohammad Ahmad Ali laughed.

"Look at the bright side. You'll have a better time in the next world, Mohammad Ahmad Ali, and you'll be rewarded tenfold."

"Do you remember the year before the famine?"

"Yes."

"That year fish was plentiful so I was able to have a wife for a while."

"Listen! Their footsteps are getting closer."

"None of them is talking. The women aren't ululating. They call this a wedding? They look like they're escorting a corpse! So lifeless! Why is that, Zahed?"

"Not all weddings have to be gay. Some of them turn out this way."

"You've got a point, Zahed."

The crowd of women entered the alley and approached the two men listlessly.

"Get up Mohammad Ahmad Ali. Let's beat the drums," said Zahed.

The women began to ululate and cheer as soon as they caught sight of the graveyard.

9

Two days later it turned cooler and the water near the shore swarmed with small fish. Zakariya and Mohammad Ahmad Ali seized their nets as they got ready to go fling them out. There, at the water's edge, they found the mullah sitting on an overturned boat with his cap and his bag, waiting.

"Good morning, Mullah," said Zakariya.

Mohammad Ahmad Ali had stopped at a distance from the dozing mullah, whose cap was pulled far over his forehead.

"What are you doing here this time of day?" the mullah sleepily responded.

"We're going fishing. Plenty of fish out today," said Zakariya.

"If we catch more than we need, we'll give you a couple of pounds," said Mohammad Ahmad Ali.

"I don't want any. I'm going off somewhere—I've some important matters to attend to," responded the mullah.

"What about your house, your wife?" demanded Zakariya.

"She'll stay. I'm leaving," murmured the mullah.

"What's she going to live on?" queried Zakariya.

"Don't worry. I've taken care of everything," answered the mullah.

"May your honor increase. It's all right by me," said Zakariya.

Mohammad Ahmad Ali pulled up his loin cloth and stepped into the water. Zakariya unfolded his fishing net and threw it over his shoulder.

"May God grant you long life," he said to the mullah, rolling up his trouser legs.

The two men wading some yards into the sea cast their nets. As the weighted nets sank, Zakariya looked over his shoulder and saw the old pickup truck stop near the mullah. The bearded driver was watching Mohammad Ahmad Ali and Zakariya, his head stretched out of the window. Two men sat next to him; all three were wearing dark glasses.

"O merciful God! Here they come again!" said Mohammad Ahmad Ali.

"Don't look at them. Mind your own work," said Zakariya.

The mullah grabbed the back of the van and hoisted himself up, joining the few men inside. He waved goodbye and Zakariya waved back. The pickup glided away noiselessly and disappeared.

"Hey, Zakariya!" cried Mohammad Ahmad Ali.

Zakariya saw his net sink and began to gather and pull it out. Mohammad Ahmad Ali pulled his out.

"Hey, Mohammad Ahmad Ali!" Zakariya exclaimed.

"Look at your net!" gasped Mohammad Ahmad Ali.

Prickly little black fish filled the nets, straining to tear loose. Frightened, the two men twisted and shook their nets hard. The fish flopped back into the sea and the men splashed back to the shore.

10

In the evening the village men sitting together in front of the mosque saw a small boat wandering over the sea, first approaching the shore, then retreating, as if afraid to come to land.

"What's she up to? Is she coming or going? What does she want to do?" said Mohammad Hajji Mostafa.

"She's not standing still. She's moving; somebody's rowing," said Mohammad Ahmad Ali.

"I wonder which village they come from," said Kadkhoda.

"Who knows!" said Saleh.

"I certainly don't!" grunted Mohammad Hajji Mostafa.

Zakariya's sister appeared, carrying a big pitcher of water. She walked past the men and moved on towards Zakariya's house. The men watched her from the corners of their eyes.

"Do you hear it?" said Mohammad Ahmad Ali.

"Hear what?" asked Zakariya, who was sitting by the coffin.

"Voices are calling from the sea," whispered Mohammad Ahmad Ali. The men listened.

"You're right. They're calling us," said Saleh.

"Let's go closer," said Kadkhoda.

They got up. When they reached the sea, the boat came toward shore. It was an old dilapidated boat, patched together with nails and strips of wire. A dead sea-bird with a head like an owl's hung from the bow. To the stern were tied two smaller boats; in each boat sat a black man, each man with a brazier and waterpipe before him. In the front boat were sitting a dozen men, most of them blind; all faced toward shore. Those who could see were sitting in front trying to keep the boat still with short strokes of the oars. A man leaning over the bow shouted, "Ahoy! Have you seen a stranger around here?"

"What did he say?" Kadkhoda asked Saleh.

"He is asking whether we've seen a stranger around here," said Saleh.

"Tell him we haven't," said Kadkhoda.

"No, we haven't seen any strangers around here," Saleh called back.

"He was a mullah. Wasn't he here?" they shouted from the boat.

"They've come after the mullah," Saleh said to the men.

"Yes, the mullah was here. He left the day before yesterday," Zakariya shouted back.

"Where did he go?" they shouted from the boat.

"He didn't say. He just left," said Zakariya.

There was a commotion on the boat.

"What did you want with him?" Zakariya shouted.

"He came to our village and got married. His wife has died at childbirth; we came to tell him," a man leaning over the bow shouted.

The village men looked at one another. No one spoke. The oarsmen pressed their oars down and the boat turned toward the horizon. They rowed faster. The two black men smoking the waterpipes watched the receding shore over their shoulders. The village men waited on the shore as the boats moved farther and farther, until each was the size of a shoe on the water.

11

First there was a commotion, then a car honking its horn. Abd al-Javad raised his head.

"It's the mullah," he shouted.

The village men who had been lying in the shade under the mosque's portico rose. Zakariya rushed to shore, where the pickup had stopped. The other men followed. The driver was watching the sea, his elbows thrust out of the window. When the men reached the car, he turned toward them and removed his glasses. He was alone. Zakariya lifted the canvas at the back of the van and looked in. There was no one inside. A big coffin, a large, full burlap sack and some onions were in one corner. Zakariya went towards the driver,

"Where's the mullah's house?" the driver asked.

"The mullah left a long time ago. You took him away yourself," said Zakariya.

"I'm looking for his house, not himself."

"In that direction," Zakariya pointed at the graveyard.

"Go tell his wife to come here. I was given a parcel to deliver to her."

"She can't walk; she is due any time now."

"Doesn't she have any relatives?"

"I'm her brother."

The driver gave Zakariya a package wrapped in black cloth.

"Give her this," he said.

Zakariya took the package. The driver started the car and drove off behind the ruins. Zakariya and the village men began to walk toward the mullah's house. On their way they came across Zakariya's wife who was fetching water from the reservoir for the mullah's wife.

12

Zakariya's sister had become ill a few days before she went into labor. Her arms and legs had swelled up and she could hardly breathe. The village women were keeping vigil, some up on the roof of Zakariya's sister's house; others were around the house. In their hands they were carrying brooms. Every few minutes they would charge at an imaginary target, shouting, "*Kish, kish!* Go away!"*

Zakariya's wife was sitting with Saleh Kamzari's wife and elder daughter just outside the room when the sick woman screamed. They rushed to her and fearfully pulled the baby into the world. It had short legs and a large head. On its back was a large mole with dark, long hair. Below the mole protruded something soft and translucent, like a cow's eye, staring.

"O Mohammad! Prophet of God! What on earth is this?" Zakariya's wife said.

"Put it down. Don't touch it. It isn't human," said Saleh's wife.

As the baby breathed, its cheeks swelled and its red, lively eyes opened

* To ward off evil spirits.

wide, staring outwards. Zakariya's wife placed it in the wicker cradle, her hands shaking.

"What shall I do?" she said.

"Keep it quiet, or the poor woman will be frightened to death," said Saleh's wife.

Zakariya's wife carried the cradle out and placed it under an old date palm. Saleh's wife and elder daughter followed her.

"Go call the women," Zakariya's wife said to Saleh's daughter, who left promptly. A few minutes later the village women rushed into the court-yard with their brooms, and gathered around the cradle.

"Look at it! Look at its finger-nails!" said Mohammad Hajji Mostafa's wife.

"Wait till you see its back. It's got an eye and another strange thing on its back," said Saleh's wife.

"I knew this was going to happen. He was deformed—you could tell his children would be deformed, too," said Kadkhoda's wife.

"When its cheeks swell up, you know, it's breathing," said Zakariya's wife.

"It doesn't look like it's breathing to me. Strange! Have you seen how a fish fills its mouth?" said Saleh's wife.

"Let's think what we should do," said Mohammad Hajji Mostafa's wife.

"What can we do?" asked Zakariya's wife.

"Place a boulder on its chest, so it stops breathing," said Saleh's wife.

"No, sister. How do you know that that isn't murder? God would punish us for it," said Kadkhoda's wife.

"Leave it alone. Let's just wait and see what happens," said Zakariya's wife.

The women bent over the cradle. The baby opened its eyes and laughed. Then, slowly, its cheeks deflated and its eyes closed.

"Thank God it's dead," said Saleh's wife.

Zakariya's wife spread a blood-stained cloth over it. The women smiled at one another, relieved.

"Let's see how the mother is faring," said Saleh's wife.

The women rushed to the room, leaving their brooms at the door. The mullah's wife lay in the middle of the room all cramped up. She had turned black from head to toe.

"O God! Look! Look what's happened!" Zakariya's wife cried.

The women approached the body nervously.

"Is she dead?" asked Kadkhoda's wife.

"Yes, Sister. Sit down and cry. Zakariya's sister has passed away," said

Saleh Kamzari's wife.

The women sat down and began to wail. Mohammad Hajji Mostafa's wife rose as she was crying, and spread a floor mat over the body. When they had had their fill of tears, Zakariya's wife said, "Now, let's go tell the men."

The wives of Mohammad Hajji Mostafa and Kadkhoda left the room, picked up their brooms at the door, and entered the graveyard through the courtyard door. The women's lamentation rose through the ventilation tower, sounding all over the village. As the women passed a clump of sabr* shrubs they saw Mohammad Ahmad Ali, Zahed and Mohammad Hajji Mostafa rushing toward the mullah's house, already carrying the coffin on their shoulders.

13

In the morning, Kadkhoda's son and a dozen youths got the boat ready and set out to look for the mullah in the nearby villages. Mohammad Ahmad Ali went along too. Zakariya stood on the shore.

"Find him any way you can. Tell him to come bury his wife," he repeated aloud.

His foot over the bow, Kadkhoda's son watched the young men push the boat backward into the sea. When the boat was well on its way, Kadkhoda's son sat down at the helm. Mohammad Ahmad Ali sat with his back to the shore, holding his head in his hands. The young men began to row with rapid strokes.

"What's wrong with you, Mohammad Ahmad Ali?" asked Kadkhoda's son.

Mohammad Ahmad Ali raised his head and stared at the sea.

"Every time someone dies I get sick. I get the shakes. I feel scared. It's always been like that. When it happens I go out to sea. The sea is good. As long as there's no earth under my feet I don't feel scared. I stop shaking. If you weren't going out to sea, I would be going myself. I would wander around a few hours, pray, fish. I would keep myself busy. I can't bear to look at the land. Even if I recover, I'll nearly die of fright as soon as my feet touch the ground. I'm afraid I'll step over the dead," he said.

*A type of aloe plant.

"God have mercy!" said Kadkhoda's son.

"Amen, O Lord of the Worlds," said Mohammad Ahmad Ali.

"It's no use going after the mullah. What good would it do even if we found him? His wife is dead; whether he comes or not it's all over with," said one of the youths.

"The point is that he's the master and he's got to bury her. If he isn't found within twenty-four hours, they'll bury her themselves," said Mohammad Ahmad Ali.

At sundown they reached a village of mud huts dispersed along a ragged shore. Near the ruins, below a fallen wall, a dozen men sat waiting for the sun to go down so that they could say their evening prayer. In the horizon, the sun resembled a carefree boat out on a long journey, surrendering itself to the waves which rose and fell, with water splashing against its hull. Kadkhoda's son now put his foot on the bow, signalling to the oarsmen to slow down. Mohammad Ahmad Ali was still sitting with his back to the shore. Kadkhoda's son yelled out. The villagers answered from the shore. The men sitting by the wall then got up and approached the water's edge.

"Ahoy! Haven't you seen a stranger around here?" Kadkhoda's son shouted.

"What stranger?" one of the men answered from the shore.

"He was a mullah. Did he show up around here?"

"Yes, the mullah was here. He married a few nights ago and left yesterday," the same man answered.

"Where did he go?"

"We have no idea."

"Well, now what shall we do?" the youths asked Kadkhoda's son.

"There isn't anything we can do," said Mohammad Ahmad Ali.

"What did you want with him?" the men asked from the shore.

"His wife is dead. We came to tell him," Kadkhoda's son answered.

The men ashore looked at one another and said nothing. Kadkhoda's son waved to the oarsmen, who raised the oars. The boat turned and set out along the red border of the sea.

THIRD STORY

It was sundown. The men had left the village and were watching the gypsies celebrate in a low lying field, with music and singing. Some of the gypsies were blacksmiths, squatting before their tents. Before them, the gypsy women danced to the sound of bagpipes, tambourines, and the kamanche.* The gypsies' low, ragged tents were pitched at the bottom of the hill. Now and then thick smoke would puff up from behind them but quickly disappear.

Kadkhoda, Zakariya, and Mohammad Hajji Mostafa, sitting on the mound, were surrounded by the rest of the village men. Zakariya was in a good mood.

"Tell Zahed to come watch them and learn how to play," he said to Kadkhoda.

"Come, Zakariya! Zahed isn't a musician. He plays the drum because he is a Black. What else can he do?" asked Kadkhoda.

"Besides, Zahed is old and poor. He's finished. If once upon a time he knew something, he doesn't now. Remember that!" said Mohammad Hajji Mostafa.

"What a good show they're putting on," said Zakariya.

"This is all they do, Zakariya. God forbid! God forbid! Their god has said if you don't sing and dance you're not my people. A gypsy once told me that if any of them goes a few days without dancing and playing music he's thrown out of the tribe and has to become an itinerant blacksmith," said Kadkhoda.

The men watched three dark, thin women dance in front of the tambourine players, waving their handkerchiefs.

"Do you want to join in, Zakariya?" asked Kadkhoda's son, who was sitting lower down on the mound.

"With the gypsies?" said Zakariya.

"Why not?" said Kadkhoda's son.

Zakariya was about to descend when he saw Mohammad Ahmad Ali breathing hard as he climbed the far side of the mound.

*A violin-like instrument.

"What's the matter with you?" Zakariya laughed.

Mohammad Ahmad Ali stopped to catch his breath.

"Abd al-Javad's wife has gone berserk," Zakariya replied.

The men turned to look at Mohammad Ahmad Ali.

"What's the matter?" Kadkhoda asked Zakariya.

"Abd al-Javad's wife has gone berserk," Zakariya repeated.

The men rose to leave; the youths watched them.

"Where are you going?" asked Kadkhoda's son.

"To the village. Abd al-Javad's wife has gone berserk and taken to her bed," said Mohammad Hajji Mostafa.

"What are you going to do?" asked Kadkhoda's son.

"You boys stay here and watch the gypsies," said Zakariya.

"If something goes wrong, come tell us," said Kadkhoda's son.

The men began to descend the hill. Mohammad Ahmad Ali took Zakariya's arm and pulled him aside.

"Hey, Zakariya, what's going to happen?" he asked.

Zakariya did not answer.

"What's going to happen? If you have any idea tell me," Mohammad Ahmad Ali repeated.

"How am I supposed to know. If something happens to her it can't be helped," said Zakariya.

"What's wrong, Zakariya? Looks like everybody is dying."

"You're so afraid of death! How are you going to die? You're afraid of death, you're afraid of the dead. Sooner or later we all have to die, don't we?"

"Sure, Zakariya. I'm not saying we shouldn't die. It's a debt we all have to pay. Sooner or later we'll all die. O save us from this earth!"

"If you don't like the earth go live on top of the water."

"I can't help it, Zakariya. Every time I hear someone is dead I am scared to death."

"In that case you'd better stop thinking about death."

"All right, Zakariya. Say something nice, so I can forget all this kind of talk."

"I can't think of anything right now. Let's go see what's up. Tonight the two of us will go out to sea and fish."

"The water will be good tonight."

"Sure. The tide will be high, very high."

They looked at the sky. On their right was a pale moon with rough edges, like fish skin dried under the sun.

"Thank God," said Mohammad Ahmad Ali.

When they reached the village, Zakariya turned to his companion.

"Hey, Mohammad Ahmad Ali, if you don't feel well don't come to Abd al-Javad's. Go to the mosque," he said.

Mohammad Ahmad Ali was only too glad to comply. He released Zakariya's arm, walked away from the men, then began to run toward the mosque. The men passed an alley and reached the village square, where torn fishing nets were heaped up. Abd al-Javad was sitting despondently, his head in his hands over his knees. When he saw the men he got up and approached them.

"What's the matter Abd al-Javad?" said Kadkhoda.

"I don't know. It seems she ate dates after childbirth, then developed a pain in her head and went berserk," said Abd al-Javad.

"When did she give birth?" asked Zakariya.

"Last night," said Abd al-Javad.

"Is the baby all right?" asked Zakariya.

"It was still-born," said Abd al-Javad.

Zakariya looked around him and was relieved to find Mohammad Ahmad Ali missing. The men squatted down in front of Abd al-Javad's house.

"What's she doing now, Abd al-Javad?" asked Mohammad Hajji Mostafa.

"The women are with her. When she's quiet my mother gives her a drink of some medicine. But when she has an attack no one can control her. She smashes things, sings, cries," said Abd al-Javad.

"Maybe seeing her baby dead affected her," said Mohammad Hajji Mostafa.

"Heaven knows," exclaimed Abd al-Javad.

"You should've kept it from her. If you had she would've been all right," said Mohammad Hajji Mostafa.

"She became ill before she found out about the baby," said Abd al-Javad.

"Have you called Zahed?" asked Kadkhoda.

"What for?" said Abd al-Javad.

"It can't hurt. He brings good luck, recites verses, plays the drum, has some skills," said Kadkhoda.

"This is all talk. Zahed would play the drum for himself and master his own spirit* if he could. Only God can help," said Abd al-Javad.

*In the original bad, i.e. a supernatural force that "rides" its subject. It can be appeased through certain rituals, among them beating the drum.

"It isn't so, Abd al-Javad. God sends the remedy as well as the disease. He is called the Most Merciful," said Mohammad Hajji Mostafa.

"I agree, but what good would come of reciting verses? I don't object to medicine and a doctor. But, if Zahed plays the drum for her, I'm sure she'll get worse," said Abd al-Javad.

"You're right, Abd al-Javad. But where are we going to find medicine and a doctor? If Isaac the Physician lived around here we could fetch him," said Kadkhoda.

"I've heard he doesn't leave Gurzeh, so the sick are taken to him. He isn't planning to return to Jerusalem any more," said Saleh Kamzari.

"What can we do? Can we take her to Gurzeh?" said Abd al-Javad.

"Why not. Sure we can," said Zakariya.

Suddenly the women in Abd al-Javad's house began to scream. The seated men turned and stared. The door swung open and the women dashed out, pushing wildly at one another, rushing to the square. The men rose.

"Go see what's wrong, Abd al-Javad," said Zakariya.

Abd al-Javad hurried into the house. The men turned their backs to the house to avoid seeing Abd al-Javad's wife, who appeared in the doorway half-naked, carrying a stick.

2

The next morning the men chained Abd al-Javad's wife and took her down to the shore so as to get her aboard the boat. The weather was fine and the sea calm.

A strange din seemed to stir the far off edge of the sea. The woman's arms and legs had been tied and she had been wrapped in a black *chador.** The men stood around her, wondering how to get her aboard, shrinking with fear each time she shrieked or moved.

"How are you going to get her into the boat?" Kadkhoda said.

"No problem. We'll get her in," said Mohammad Ahmad Ali.

"You've wrapped the poor woman so tight she can't move a joint," said Kadkhoda.

*A veil; a large triangular piece of cloth covering the head and the body.

"Don't worry. Abd al-Javad will carry her into the boat on his back," said Zakariya.

"Hey, Abd al-Javad, aren't you afraid to put her on your back?" said Mohammad Ahmad Ali.

"Afraid? Nobody is afraid of his own wife, why should I be?" retorted Abd al-Javad.

The men looked at Mohammad Ahmad Ali and Saleh glared at him. Mohammad Ahmad Ali sneaked behind Zakariya.

"Hurry up, before the water rises," said Mohammad Hajji Mostafa.

Abd al-Javad stepped closer to his wife and took hold of the chains around her arms.

"Hey Zakariya, can you hold her legs, so she won't push me into the water?" he said.

Zakariya and the rest of the men helped Abd al-Javad take his wife on his back. Zakariya held her legs, which trembled in the *chador*.

"Keep going, Abd al-Javad. Keep going. Don't be afraid," he said.

Kadkhoda's son and another youth stepped into the water, escorting Abd al-Javad to the boat. The latter walked hurriedly, splashing Zakariya with water. Zakariya was holding the patient's legs. Each time she shrieked he threw his head back and held her more tightly.

"She could jump into the water," said Mohammad Ahmad Ali to Mohammad Hajji Mostafa.

"Don't worry. May it please God she won't," said Mohammad Hajji Mostafa.

"It's no good taking his wife to Isaac. After all, Isaac is a Jew. He's not pure of heart,"* said Kadkhoda.

"Well, Kadkhoda, in matters like this you and I have no say. The husband is in charge and it has to be he who decides. Abd al-Javad is set on Isaac. With God's help she'll recover," said Mohammad Hajji Mostafa.

"Look, Kadkhoda! Look, Mohammad Hajji Mostafa! Look how they're carrying her onto the boat, as if they were putting her into a coffin," said Mohammad Ahmad Ali.

The men watched in silence from the shore. Abd al-Javad and Zakariya were on board, pulling the patient in as though she were a corpse, while Kadkhoda's son and another youth held her tightly.

"Tell Abd al-Javad's mother to come aboard," Zakariya cried from the boat.

Mohammad Ahmad Ali stepped into the water and pulled his small tin

---

* In the original, *nafas-i pak nadareh.*

skiff ashore. Abd al-Javad's mother got in and Mohammad Ahmad Ali pulled the skiff out to join the boat, careful to keep it from capsizing. He and Abd al-Javad's mother then stepped over into the larger boat.

"Hey Abd al-Javad! Hey Zakariya! Isaac is greedy. If he tries to take all you've got, don't be taken in," Kadkhoda called out from the shore.

No one answered. Only the chains jingled out from the sea.

3

At high tide they disembarked at Gurzeh. The weather was fine, but the sea was tumultuous. Mohammad Ahmad Ali and Zakariya went to the village and fetched a rubber-wheeled cart drawn by two donkeys. They helped Abd al-Javad's wife and mother to get in. Then the carter got in. The men walked beside the cart, along the shore, until they reached the road that led them to the village. The people of Gurzeh were sitting outside their doors when the group reached the square. A sayyid * left one of the shacks to take them some water. Zakariya, Abd al-Javad and Kadkhoda's son drank, but Mohammad Ahmad Ali did not. They set out again, crossing an alley flanked by mud houses and jagged walls. The path was uphill, so the carter got off and walked with the men.

"Where's his house, then? We're outside the village," said Zakariya.

"Past the fortress," said the carter.

"In the desert?"

"Yes. He's built himself a house out there."

"Doesn't he come to the village?"

"No. He stays home all the time."

"Who does his chores?"

"Two Blacks, a man and a woman."

"Are they Jews, too?"

"No, they're from the Island. The man's name is Khamiz, the woman's Hajar."

"Where does he see his patients?"

"He's built shacks all around his house. The patients sleep in the shacks."

---

*A descendant of the Prophet, usually identified by his green turban or cummerbund.

"Do they get well?"

"Sure they do."

"Does he know our language?"

"Of course he does."

The men walked in silence until they reached the ruins of a fortress surrounded by gigantic green rocks. Chains jingled and a baby coughed in the fortress as the cart turned around it and reached the level plain near the shore, where Isaac's house was located. The house was surrounded by dilapidated straw shacks at the entrances of which hung tattered curtains. People could be seen in some of the shacks through gaps in the straw mats. The cart stopped before the house. Zakariya and the carter helped Abd al-Javad lift up his wife onto his shoulders. They knocked and an old Black opened the door. He wore white trousers and there was a chain around his neck.

"Is Isaac up?" the carter said.

"He is," said the Black.

"We have a patient."

The Black looked out.

"Bring her in," he said, pointing to the courtyard.

Abd al-Javad entered, followed by Zakariya and the rest of the party, with Mohammad Ahmad Ali and the carter behind them. It was a small square courtyard with two tall slender doors, one of them padlocked. There were no windows. Abd al-Javad placed his wife on the porch. The Black went inside the house through the unlocked door.

"See how she's doing, Abd al-Javad. She hasn't moved since we got off the boat," said Zakariya.

Abd al-Javad motioned to his mother, who unwrapped the patient's black chador and examined her. She was still breathing. The men sat on the ground, except for Mohammad Ahmad Ali. The Black returned and told them to take the patient inside.

Zakariya and Abd al-Javad carried her in.

"Sit down," the carter told Mohammad Ahmad Ali.

"What's he going to do to her?" said Mohammad Ahmad Ali as he sat down.

"Heaven knows. How am I supposed to know?" demanded the carter.

"Is he in there?" Mohammad Ahmad Ali asked, pointing at the room.

"You mean in the one that's locked?" said the carter.

"What's it like? Why is it locked?" asked Mohammad Ahmad Ali.

"Don't worry about these things. The Black will bring her here right away," said Kadkhoda's son.

"These two rooms are connected," said the carter.

Zakariya stuck his head out of the door and called Abd al-Javad's mother. Mohammad Ahmad Ali looked around him apprehensively and began to pray. Abd al-Javad's mother squeezed through the half-opened door. The room was dark and damp, the floor covered with straw mats. High up the wall between the two rooms was a small window with red curtains; below it was another window, large enough for a man to crawl through. An old black woman holding a big knife sat in the far corner next to a pail of water. She would take live crabs out of the pail, put them on the bloody rock in front of her, wait until they moved their claws, then laugh and split them with the knife. When the crabs stopped moving she would drop them into a big jar. In the opposite corner was a pile of hay under which something was twitching. Every few minutes the black woman would walk to the pile and strike it with a stick. Then the pile would stop moving.

They untied the patient. The old black man gathered the chains, tossed them into the courtyard, and returned to the window. He stood thinking for a while, watching Zakariya and Abd al-Javad sternly, making them fidget nervously. He then knocked at the window. A gruff cough answered. The Black sat down on the floor, gathering his arms around his knees. The pile of dry hay twitched again. They all stood there.

"What is it?" someone called from the other room.

"They've brought a woman," said the Black.

"Is she sick?" said the voice.

"Very sick," said the Black.

Zakariya and Abd al-Javad huddled together. The live crabs clawed at the pail. The old black woman knocked at the pail with a stick and the clawing stopped. Then she moved closer to the crowd. After a few moments the red curtain slowly moved to one side and an old man's big, boney, bearded face appeared in the window.

"If he asks anything will you answer him for me?" Abd al-Javad said to Zakariya.

"All right, I will," said Zakariya.

"Which one is the patient?" asked the old man, his eyes and lips almost hidden under his thick eyebrows and beard.

Zakariya pointed at Abd al-Javad's wife.

"Move over so I can see her," said the old man.

The men moved away from the patient.

"She isn't dead, is she?" the old man asked.

"No, she fainted in the boat," said Zakariya.

"How do you know she isn't dead, you ignoramus?" said the old man.

"She's breathing," said Zakariya.

"Hey, Khamiz, see if she's alive," the old man shouted.

Khamiz crawled to the patient and motioned to the old black woman. Together they stretched the patient out on the floor. Then Khamiz measured her hand by hand from head to toe, whispered in the black woman's ear, then went to the window.

"She's alive," he said.

"Good," the old man smiled, dropping the curtain and disappearing. The old black man and woman jumped up and down for joy and kissed.

"What's happened? Why are they acting so strange?" said Abd al-Javad.

"I don't understand," said Zakariya.

"Hush! Don't talk," said Khamiz.

"Why not?" said Zakariya.

"Be quiet. He's trying to think," said Khamiz, pointing at the curtain.

They fell silent. The old man drew the curtain aside again, this time puffing a waterpipe hurriedly and sending the thick smoke into the room.

"What's he going to do to her?" Zakariya said to Abd al-Javad.

"Quiet! Don't talk," Khamiz ordered.

"Did you bring money?" asked the old man, squeezing the reed in his fist. Abd al-Javad took out his money bag and gave it to Zakariya.

"Yes, we did," said Zakariya.

"Let me see," said the old man.

Zakariya handed the money bag to the Black, who gave it to the old man. The old man appraised the bag.

"This won't cure her," he said, tossing the bag into the room and dropping the red curtain.

The crabs twitched in the pail.

"What shall we do?" said Abd al-Javad.

"I don't know," said Zakariya.

"We're stuck, Zakariya. We've got to pay him what he wants. Give me whatever money you've got. I'll pay you back when we get home," said Abd al-Javad.

Zakariya put his money bag over Abd al-Javad's and gave the bags to the Black, who then knocked again. The old man appeared in the window, took the bags, appraised them and smiled. Zakariya and Abd al-Javad looked at each other.

"How many are you?" the old man asked.

"Six or seven," said Zakariya.

"Give them a big shack," the old man said to Khamiz, moved aside, then dropped the curtain. Khamiz opened the lower window and the black woman hurriedly picked the jar of chopped crabs and crawled through the window into the old man's room.

4

The dilapidated shack provided little shelter against the cold wind blowing from the sea. It was stormy. The sea raged, high waves burst in the dark, and the wind beat against the water. The sounds of chains rattling across the horizon filled the night. Unfamiliar laughter cracked the darkness and muffled coughs came from the shacks. Everything was in deepest darkness.

Now and then, when the moon burst through the clouds, a head would stick out of a shack, look around and disappear.

Abd al-Javad's wife and mother were lying down on the dais in the shack, asleep. The rest of the party were sleeping sitting down, except for Mohammad Ahmad Ali, who paced about, unable to fall asleep. Whenever the moon shone, he would thrust his head out and look around. About midnight the wind became boisterous, waking Zakariya.

"Why didn't you sleep?" he asked Mohammad Ahmad Ali.

"Doesn't let me sleep."

"Who doesn't let you?"

Mohammad Ahmad Ali pointed outside. Zakariya stuck his head out. A big cart was passing between the shacks, headed for the village.

"Who were they?" Zakariya turned to Mohammad Ahmad Ali.

"I'm scared," Mohammad Ahmad Ali said.

"Scared of what? Let's go out. You'll see there's nothing to be scared of."

Outside, the wind spun around the shacks, fluttering the mats and the front curtains.

"Where are we going, Zakariya?" Mohammad Ahmad Ali said.

"We'll take a walk by the sea."

They reached the sea after a long walk and continued along the shore. The rolling waves painted the sea purple with their sparkles and flames.

Zakariya and Mohammad Ahmad Ali slowly approached Isaac's house as they continued to watch the sea. Mohammad Ahmad Ali walked laboriously, hiding behind Zakariya.

"Hey, Zakariya, look at that!" he exclaimed, pointing at the horizon.

"Look at what?" Zakariya stopped.

"A ship! Looks like a mountain! When did it get here? Where is it from?"

"Where is it?"

"Over there."

"You've gone mad. That's not a ship. It's the tide rising."

Mohammad Ahmad Ali was reassured. They began to walk again.

"Hey, Zakariya!" Mohammad Ahmad Ali shouted after a few steps.

"What the hell is it now?"

"You can see *that*, can't you?"

Zakariya saw a big rowboat approaching the shore. They sneaked behind a shack to watch the boat.

Slowly, the boat reached the shore. First Isaac the Physician stepped ashore, looking very tall in his long, white cloak. He was followed by Khamiz and Hajar, who lifted a strange looking corpse out of the boat. The corpse's legs and arms resembled a human's, but its head was elongated and weird. Zakariya and Mohammad Ahmad Ali ran back to the shack.

The shack was hot. Everybody was asleep, except for the carter, who had awakened and was smoking.

5

At dawn, Khamiz and Hajar came for the patient. Everybody was awake and Abd al-Javad's mother was pouring water down the patient's throat.

"Are you up?" asked Hajar.

"Yes, we are," said the carter.

"Bring her out," said Hajar.

"Out where?" said Mohammad Ahmad Ali.

"Bring her out. He wants to start," said Khamiz.

"Is he up already?" the carter asked.

"He's always up. Never sleeps," said Khamiz.

Mohammad Ahmad Ali nudged Zakariya, who turned and glared at him. A hot wind carrying the sting of the sun rattled the shack.

Hajar and Khamiz entered the shack and looked around.

"Hurry up," Hajar said.

"If it gets late he'll take offense and won't do a thing for you," said Khamiz.

"Why won't he?" said Zakariya.

"That's the way he is. He's old and impatient," Khamiz said.

Zakariya and Mohammad Ahmad Ali looked at each other and got up. Abd al-Javad carried the patient on his back; Zakariya and the rest followed him.

"Hey, Zakariya, I think I'd better stay here. I don't have to come, do I? I'll look after the shack," Mohammad Ahmad Ali said.

"The shack needs no looking after," said the carter.

"Why don't you stay too? There's nothing you could do. So stay with me," Mohammad Ahmad Ali said to the carter.

"I can't. I've got to see what happens," said the carter, leaving.

The wind had piled a sandhill between the shacks and Isaac's house, and they had to go round it to the house. Around the courtyard there were a few casks, some strange receptacles, a bundle of straps and chains, a few buckets, and two coffins. There was a big fire on one of the porches. Abd al-Javad and Zakariya carried the patient into one of the rooms. The rest sat in the courtyard, except for Abd al-Javad's mother, who was about to follow Zakariya when Hajar called after her.

"Stop! He doesn't let women in."

"How come he lets you in?" Abd al-Javad's mother protested.

"I'm black and I work for him," Hajar said.

Abd al-Javad and Zakariya stretched out the patient on the floor and sat down. The room was full of copper vessels of all sizes, a variety of swords, begging-pans, and incense burners. At the front of the room there was a big copper basin brimming with glowing charcoal. Hajar stirred the fire and tossed a bundle of weeds over the flames. As a strong odor filled the room, she spread a white cloth on the floor at the patient's head and placed a low stool over it. When she was done, she nodded at Khamiz, who knocked at the window and sat down by the wall. Then Isaac lifted the curtain, looked into the room and smiled, dropping the curtain. Hajar motioned to Khamiz, who opened the small window and crawled to a corner. Zakariya and Abd al-Javad stooped to look into Isaac's room, Khamiz shook his finger at them and they sat up straight. A few moments later Isaac crawled into the room through the window, then stood up straight, his white cloak dragging on the floor, a long string of prayer beads in his hand. His many wrinkles covered his eyes and his combed beard reached his belly. Zakariya and Abd al-Javad rose and stood in a corner. Slowly, Isaac walked to the patient and sat on the stool, spreading his legs. He nodded. Hajar and Khamiz dragged the patient onto the cloth. Hajar removed the patient's *chador* from her face and took off her veil. The patient's eyes were open, staring blankly at the ceiling. Isaac bent over and looked into her eyes. She moaned and moved her hands. Isaac nodded. Hajar fetched a rosewater bottle and poured a few drops on the patient's lips. She moved and gathered up her legs. Isaac smiled and Khamiz crawled over to Hajar, who handed a large pair of scissors to Isaac.

Isaac cut the hair on the patient's right temple. Hajar reached for a copper bowl, took a big, live crab, and dropped it on the patient's temple. The crab was motionless at first, but when the moisture on its shell dried up, it pierced the skin of the temple with its claws. Hajar poured salt over the crab, which began to twitch.

"What's she doing?" Abd al-Javad asked Zakariya.

Isaac glared at them. Khamiz and Hajar opened the door and forced them out. In the courtyard, Zakariya and Abd al-Javad joined the carter.

"What was he doing?" Abd al-Javad's mother asked.

Zakariya shrugged and Abd al-Javad's mother asked again, "You didn't see what he was doing?"

"He was busy," said Abd al-Javad, lowering his head over his knees.

They all listened. They heard the sound of chopping. The door opened and Khamiz walked into the courtyard, his sleeves rolled up. He went to one of the casks and smelled its contents; then went to the next, smelled it, and filled a bowl with a black liquid and went back to the room, shutting the door behind him.

"What was that?" said Abd al-Javad's mother.

"I couldn't tell," said Abd al-Javad.

"What about you, Zakariya? Could you see what it was?" asked Abd al-Javad's mother.

"Probably something he uses," replied Zakariya.

They heard Abd al-Javad's wife moaning inside.

"Abd al-Javad, go take a look. See what's going on," Abd al-Javad's mother said.

"He won't let us in," Abd al-Javad said.

The door opened and Hajar entered the courtyard hastily, picked up a broad knife and a long, narrow vessel and rushed back, shutting the door. The sound of laughter and coughing filled the air. Someone sang and then Hajar laughed and a few moments later a man's cough was heard.

"O Merciful God!" exclaimed Abd al-Javad.

The patient moaned and Abd al-Javad's mother began to cry.

"Don't cry. Don't make any noise," Abd al-Javad said to his mother. The door opened. Khamiz went to one of the casks, soaked a white cloth in a yellow fluid, and returned to the room, shutting the door.

The sea thundered and raged all around the house; there was something strange in the air. Everything fluttered. The courtyard swayed like a boat adrift.

"I'm feeling dizzy," Abd al-Javad's mother said.

"Lie down. You'll feel better," Zakariya said.

"I can't lie down," Abd al-Javad's mother said.

"If you can't, then don't," said Abd al-Javad.

"How come they haven't finished yet?" said Abd al-Javad's mother.

"How long does it take?" Zakariya asked the carter.

"I don't know. Only he knows," said the carter.

Hajar and Khamiz left the room; Khamiz carried the copper basin into the yard and emptied the burned-up ash-covered charcoal. Hajar filled it with fresh glowing charcoal and they returned to the room. The sea had grown more clamorous. The ground swayed wildly and the courtyard was filled with dust, when suddenly the patient shrieked, bringing them to themselves. Abd al-Javad's mother burst into tears. The carter left through the courtyard door. A few moments later, Hajar and Khamiz entered the courtyard and carried one of the coffins into the room.

6

Around sunset, the storm diminished and the waves subsided. The moon rose. Most of the shacks were uprooted by the wind, their debris scattered over the sand or down to the water. In one shack lay Mohammad Ahmad Ali, running a fever. The rest of the party sat outside on the shore, waiting for the carter to return from the village so he could take them to their boat. Suddenly they saw a huge ship looming on the horizon. It had colorful pennants and copper cannons on both ends of the deck. Khamiz and Hajar ran out of the house, singing and dancing, playing the tambourine. Zakariya rushed to them and caught Khamiz by the shoulder.

"What's up? Where's that ship from? What does it want?" he asked.

"It comes from Jerusalem, to fetch Isaac," Khamiz said, trembling with joy and excitement.

Over the deck, the cannons were fired again and again.

FOURTH STORY

In the evening Saleh Kamzari and Kadkhoda's son rowed along the shore in their skiff to collect the driftwood that the previous night's rough sea had driven to the shoreline.

"I can never figure the sea out," Saleh said, pulling the driftwood toward the skiff with an old oar. "I don't know what she's like. If everybody put their heads together they still wouldn't know where all this driftwood has come from. There's something about the sea which isn't straight, which doesn't show its true face. One day she's got everything, the next day nothing. As if she's teasing you. You see all this driftwood now? In another minute, maybe, you won't find even a single piece."

"That's why they call her the sea," said Kadkhoda's son.

"Come to think of it, everything on land is from the sea. Nothing scares the sea, but she scares everybody."

Kadkhoda's son was bored.

"Come on! Grab all the wood you can and quit worrying about these things," he said.

Offended, Saleh tossed the oar on top of the pile of driftwood in the skiff and took a cigarette out. He glanced at the shore.

"Hey! Hey! Look over there," he exclaimed.

A small child was walking away from the village in long strides.

"Do you see that child?" said Saleh.*

"Whose kid is that?"

"I don't know. It walks just like a grown up."

"It's a long way from the village. Maybe it's from somewhere else."

"Like where?"

"Heaven knows. Maybe it belongs to the gypsies or the nomads."

"What gypsies? It isn't the right season."

"What do you think we should do?"

"Let's catch it."

*Since the child's sex is not stated in the original, in the translation words like *he, she, boy,* and *girl* have been avoided in referring to *it.*

"We can't row the skiff ashore."

"Then swim to the shore and catch it," Saleh said, taking the oar and pushing aside the driftwood which had accumulated around the skiff. Kadkhoda's son pulled off his shirt and jumped into the water, pushing his way through the driftwood and holding his head out of the water as he swam toward the shore. Saleh squatted on the pile of driftwood in the boat, staring out at the child striding away and Kadkhoda's son swimming toward it.

Kadkhoda's son reached the shore a few steps from the child, noticing its thin bi-colored shirt, its frizzy hair and translucent skin which glittered in the sun. With a shinbone tucked under its right arm, the child strode on, ignoring the noises behind it.

Kadkhoda's son whistled. The child hurried on without looking back. Kadkhoda's son walked faster, made a 180 degree turn, and shot in front of the child, who stopped. Kadkhoda's son stopped, too. They eyed each other for a few moments.

"Where are you heading?" Kadkhoda's son studied the child's round face and large eyes.

The child said nothing.

"Whose kid are you?"

The child backed away, looking scared.

"Are you scared? What are you scared of?" Kadkhoda's son said.

The child stopped, frowning. Kadkhoda's son smiled to alleviate the child's fear. The child eyed him carefully and switched the bone under his left arm. Kadkhoda's son stepped forward slowly. The child did not move. Kadkhoda's son knelt down on the sand, grasped the child in his arms, and rose. They stared each other in the eye.

"Where are you coming from?" Kadkhoda's son asked.

The child said nothing.

"Where are you headed?" asked Kadkhoda's son.

The child puckered up its lips, about to cry.

"Whose kid are you? Who's your father?" Kadkhoda's son asked.

The child smiled. Kadkhoda's son smiled back.

"What's this under your arm?" Kadkhoda's son asked.

The child squirmed around to look back at the sea, which made a muffled clamor.

"Cat got your tongue?" Kadkhoda's son said.

The child frowned again, about to cry.

"Don't. I'm not going to hurt you. Don't frown," Kadkhoda's son said.

"Hello! Hello!" Saleh called out from the boat.

"What's the matter?" Kadkhoda's son called back.

Saleh pointed to the skiff and Kadkhoda's son lifted the child to his back and stepped into the water. After a few steps, the current swept him up and he began to swim. The child grasped him by the head tightly and swung his legs in the water. When the two reached the skiff Saleh bent over and lifted the child into the boat. Kadkhoda's son clambered in. The two stared at the child.

"What a strange one!" exclaimed Kadkhoda's son.

"Just see its eyes," said Saleh.

Kadkhoda's son bent over the child.

"Yes, they aren't the same color," he said.

"Where is it from?"

"It won't talk, won't say a word."

Saleh lifted up the child and sat it down on top of the pile of firewood.

"What should we do with it?" he said.

"I don't think it's from our village—we don't have a strange kid like this."

"Why, do you know every kid in the village?"

"I do. You think we should take it to the village?"

"What else can we do? Toss it into the sea?"

They made a turn and rowed toward their village. The sea had begun to ebb, sucking the driftwood out toward the horizon.

"Be careful that it doesn't fall into the water," Saleh said.

Kadkhoda's son lifted the child, dozing on its driftwood nest and placed it softly, still asleep, on the bottom of the skiff.

2

When they reached the shore, the villagers' skiffs and rowboats were returning from the sea. Men and women were unloading the driftwood, and Zakariya and Mohammad Ahmad Ali were busy weighing it by the steelyard. Kadkhoda was sitting on an overturned skiff, saying his beads.

Taking the child in his arms, Saleh scrambled from the skiff. Kadkhoda's son, grabbing the anchor's rope, twisted it and threw the anchor over the sand, then jumped into the water. He and Saleh walked ashore shoulder to shoulder.

"Hope you're not too tired, Saleh," Abd al-Javad greeted them; then, seeing the child, he stepped closer, staring.

"Hey, what's this, Saleh?" he said.

"Oh, some kid," Saleh said.

"Hey, Kadkhoda! Hey, Mohammad Hajji Mostafa! Hey, Zahed, hey, everybody—Saleh has brought a child from the sea!" he cried out wide-eyed.

The villagers ran to Saleh and Kadkhoda's son, and, gathering around them, stared at the child, who seemed perfectly at ease in Saleh's arms.

"Hey, look at the kid! Look at the kid!" Abd al-Javad said, jumping up and down excitedly.

"It's from the sea, is it? Belongs to the sea?" Mohammad Ahmad Ali said, standing apart from the rest.

"Where did you catch it?" Kadkhoda asked.

"But it's wearing clothes. It can't be from the sea," Mohammad Hajji Mostafa said.

Zakariya arrived at the scene and pushed his way through the crowd.

"What a nice color it has. Look at the shade of its eyes," he said, rubbing the child's cheeks.

"Tell us the truth. Where did you find it?" Mohammad Hajji Mostafa said.

"It was walking over the water. I caught it," Saleh said.

"He's lying. Saleh Kamzari is lying," Zakariya said.

"What should we lie for? Didn't we come from the sea?" Saleh said.

"Take it back to the sea. The child of the sea brings bad luck," Mohammad Ahmad Ali said.

"Tell the truth. I'm afraid Mohammad Ahmad Ali will get sick with fright again,"* said Zakariya.

"We found it on the other shore," said Kadkhoda's son.

Relieved, the villagers stepped closer.

"Well, now, whose kid is it?" Kadkhoda said.

"It doesn't belong to our village," said Saleh.

"Could it belong to the gypsies?" Zakariya asked.

"There's no sign of the gypsies yet," Kadkhoda's son said.

"Then where is it from? Where did it come from?" Zakariya said.

"Heaven knows," said Kadkhoda's son.

"What was it doing when you saw it?" Mohammad Hajji Mostafa asked.

"Just plodding along," said Saleh.

"You mean it can walk?" Abd al-Javad said.

"Why shouldn't it?" Saleh said, putting the child down.

* In the original, "bad jun misheh," i.e. becomes possessed by a supernatural power.

The villagers opened a path. The child tucked the bone under its arm and rushed toward the village. The villagers followed.

"How weird! Look at the way it walks!" said Mohammad Hajji Mostafa.

"Yes, but it can't talk," Saleh said.

"How can that be? A child that walks can talk as well," said Zakariya.

"Well, this one can't," said Saleh.

"It keeps going. Someone go catch it," said Kadkhoda.

Kadkhoda's son caught up with the child, lifted it into his arms, and returned to the crowd, which opened a path for him. He sat on the driftwood and put the child down between his legs.

A woman gave a piece of bread to Saleh.

"Give it some bread. Let's see if it knows how to eat," she said.

Saleh gave the bread to the child who began to gnaw at it.

Relieved, the villagers stepped closer.

"What do you think we should do?" Kadkhoda said.

"Someone's got to take care of it," said Zakariya.

"Who?" said Kadkhoda.

"Someone who doesn't have any kids, who's childless," said Zakariya.

"Everyone in the village has got kids," said Mohammad Hajji Mostafa.

"That's no problem. We'll take turns caring for it, until its parents turn up," said Abd al-Javad.

"Not bad, Abd al-Javad. Who'll take care of it tonight?" said Kadkhoda.

"You. The first night it'll be Kadkhoda's guest," said Zakariya

Kadkhoda considered the offer.

"Fine, I accept," he said.

The sun had set and it was getting dark. The villagers rose to return to the village. Saleh Kamzari gave the child to Kadkhoda's son, who took it in his arms. All began walking toward the village. Mohammad Ahmad Ali caught up with Saleh.

"Hey, Saleh, Zakariya is lying. He doesn't want to tell the truth. I'm scared and full of misgiving. Where did you really find this kid?" he said.

"To tell you the truth, I don't know where we got it either," Saleh said.

3

That night they took the child to Kadkhoda's. Kadkhoda's wife kneaded the dough in the trough and baked it. Kadkhoda, his son, and

Mohammad Ahmad Ali gathered around the child, who was sitting beside the wall, stretching its legs toward the lamp. The sea was rough; the wind beat against the doors and walls. Kadkhoda had shut the windows and the wooden shutters to protect the lamp from the wind.

"What should we do with it now?" Kadkhoda said after supper.

"Put it to sleep," Kadkhoda's wife said.

"It looks so snug, as if it has no intention of ever sleeping," Kadkhoda said.

"I wish it'd say a couple of words, tell us something. Too bad it doesn't laugh, doesn't cry, doesn't talk," said Kadkhoda's son.

"You call that bad? The quieter the child the better," said Kadkhoda's wife.

"What's good about that?" said Kadkhoda's son.

"Would you rather it cried and carried on?" said Kadkhoda's wife.

"No, but it's no good this way either. It just sits there like a grown up, staring at you. Enough to give you the creeps!" grumbled Kadkhoda's son.

The wind raged more loudly and there was a knock at the door.

"There's someone out there," Kadkhoda's wife said.

Kadkhoda's son sprang up to open the door—there were Mohammad Hajji Mostafa's wife and daughter-in-law.

"Welcome! Please come in," Kadkhoda's wife said.

"We came to see the guest," said Mohammad Hajji Mostafa's wife.

They entered, bent over the child and stared it in the face, then sat by the lamp. Kadkhoda rose and went to the bath* to sleep and Mohammad Ahmad Ali sat apart from the women.

"Do you know the kid?" Kadkhoda's wife asked.

"No, I don't," said Mohammad Hajji Mostafa's daughter-in-law.

"It acts just like a grown up," Mohammad Ahmad Ali said from the corner of the room.

"What are you going to do with it?" said Mohammad Hajji Mostafa's wife.

"Nothing. Tonight, it'll stay here. Tomorrow I'll send it over to your house," said Kadkhoda's wife.

The wind raged more fiercely and there was a knock at the door.

"Company," said Kadkhoda's wife.

Kadkhoda's son answered the door, and Saleh's wife and daughter entered.

"Welcome! Welcome! Come in," said Kadkhoda's wife.

* Generally in the cellar, the coolest place in the summer.

"We came to see the kid," said Saleh's wife.

They sat beside Mohammad Hajji Mostafa's wife and daughter-in-law.

"Did Saleh tell you how they found it?" Kadkhoda's wife said.

"More or less. I came to see what the kid looks like," said Saleh's wife.

"Look at its eyes!" Mohammad Hajji Mostafa's daughter-in-law said. All bent over the child and looked.

"See the Lord's wonderful work?" said Kadkhoda's wife.

"Where do you think it is from?" said Saleh's wife.

"Nobody knows. Either the desert or the sea," said Mohammad Hajji Mostafa's wife.

"What are you going to do with it?" said Saleh's wife.

"Tonight, it'll stay here; tomorrow, at Mohammad Hajji Mostafa's; the day after that at yours," said Kadkhoda's wife.

The wind raged wildly; there was a knock at the door.

"Company again," said Kadkhoda's wife.

Kadkhoda's son opened the door to Abd al-Javad's mother.

"Come on in," said Kadkhoda's wife.

Abd al-Javad's mother entered.

"Hello. I came to see if it's true they brought a kid from the sea," she said.

"Yes, it's true. Come and see," said Kadkhoda's son.

Abd al-Javad's mother stepped closer, bent over and looked the child over, then sat beside Saleh's daughter.

"Doesn't it look strange?" Mohammad Hajji Mostafa's wife asked Abd al-Javad's mother.

"Just like a doll. Won't stir a limb," Abd al-Javad's mother said.

"Just like a grown up," said Mohammad Hajji Mostafa's daughter-in-law.

"Look at its eyes," Mohammad Ahmad Ali, who was sitting in the dark, suggested to Abd al-Javad's mother.

"Tonight it'll stay here, tomorrow night at Mohammad Hajji Mostafa's, the night after that at Saleh's, and the night after that at yours," said Kadkhoda's wife.

The wind raged more fiercely; there was another knock at the door.

"How nice! More company!" said Kadkhoda's wife.

Kadkhoda's son answered the door. There was no one outside. Only the wind burst in and blew out the lamp.

4

The sun had risen, but the men had not yet returned from the sea. Kadkhoda's wife took the child to Mohammad Hajji Mostafa's house. Mohammad Hajji Mostafa's wife was cooking cattle-feed when she heard Kadkhoda's wife outside and went to the door.

"I've brought you company," said Kadkhoda's wife.

"May your hand never ache for the favor," Mohammad Hajji Mostafa's wife said.

She took the child by the hand and pulled it inside.

"You can't imagine what a nuisance it was last night. It wouldn't sleep a wink, or let us sleep. It kept pacing up and down the room, looking for a way to get out," Kadkhoda's wife said.

"So what did you do?" Mohammad Hajji Mostafa's wife asked.

"Early in the morning when the men went out to sea they tied its arms and legs and stuck it in a trunk. I had to untie it to bring it over here."

"Maybe it was hungry?"

"No, it wasn't. It just wanted to get out. Every time the wind blew it got excited and tried to get out."

Mohammad Hajji Mostafa's wife gazed at the child and the woman.

"I hope it'll behave tonight," she said.

"I hope so too," Kadkhoda's wife said before she left.

Mohammad Hajji Mostafa's wife took the child by the hand and led it to the shade. The cattle-feed was boiling in the tin pot and the air was filling with the bitter smell of burning wood and date pits. She sat the child down by the wall and went over to stir the pot. The child remained motionless, examining its surroundings. Its eyes had grown larger, filling half its face.

Mohammad Hajji Mostafa's wife crouched on the ground by the fire, gazing at the child.

"Hey, little one, why are you looking like that?" she said.

The child did not answer.

"We're all alone. Come whisper in my ear who you belong to and where you're from."

The child did not answer, but went to the woman and sat beside her, watching the short wings of fire reaching the pot. The woman went over to the pot, spooned out some cattle-feed on a piece of wood and placed it before the child.

A cow lowed behind the wall and the child began to eat.

5

Late that night Mohammad Hajji Mostafa's wife answered a knock at the door to find a gypsy couple standing outside. She could see a man smoking and a woman sitting out there in the gloom, looking through a large saddle bag. Mohammad Hajji Mostafa's wife rushed back inside.

"Hey, Hajji, they've come for the kid, come to take it home," she yelled.

Mohammad Hajji Mostafa, who had just fallen asleep, went to the door. The couple were waiting in the narrow hallway.

"Hello! Welcome! Come in," Mohammad Hajji Mostafa said.

The couple entered without a word. Mohammad Hajji Mostafa's wife lit and carried the lamp to the parlor. The gypsies sat down leaning their backs against the wall. Mohammad Hajji Mostafa opened the window to let the cool air in. He sat before the man.

"So you finally showed up," he said.

The man looked at Mohammad Hajji Mostafa and then at his wife and laughed.

"You're probably very happy, no? Well, after all, we're delivering the child to you safe and sound, to take it home," Mohammad Hajji Mostafa said.

The man looked at the woman; they both laughed.

"Could you give us a drop of water?" the man asked.

Mohammad Hajji Mostafa's wife went to the bath and came back with a large glass of water. The couple drank and put the empty glass by the lamp.

"The child didn't sleep last night and is soundly asleep now. We'll wake it up when you're ready to leave," said Mohammad Hajji Mostafa's wife.

The couple looked at each other and said nothing.

"Saleh Kamzari and Kadkhoda's son found your child when they were out at sea," said Mohammad Hajji Mostafa.

"Saleh Kamzari?" the man said.

The woman turned her face to the wall, her shoulders shaking as she laughed.

"Do you know Saleh Kamzari?" Mohammad Hajji Mostafa asked.

"No," the man said.

"How about Kadkhoda's son?" Mohammad Hajji Mostafa said.

"Kadkhoda's son?" the man said, covering his face with his hands, laughing.

Mohammad Hajji Mostafa laughed too.

"So you don't know him either," he said.

The couple rose.

"Let me fetch the kid," Mohammad Hajji Mostafa's wife said.

She went to the next room but before she returned the gypsies opened the door and disappeared in the dark, laughing.

6

When the sun rose Mohammad Hajji Mostafa's wife took the child to Saleh Kamzari's house. Saleh's wife had gone to fetch water from the reservoir and his daughter was baking bread in the hearth.

Mohammad Hajji Mostafa's wife let go of the child in the courtyard and sat beside Saleh's daughter.

"It's your turn today. I brought the child over to stay with you," she said.

"My mother isn't feeling well. I don't think she's going to take the child," said Saleh's daughter.

"She said she would."

"She's in a lot of pain. How is she supposed to take care of the kid?"

"Then you take care of it. You're all right, aren't you?"

"I've got to look after my mother."

"Well, let's wait for your mother. Give the child a piece of bread."

Saleh's daughter cut a piece of bread and gave it to the child. A few moments later, Saleh's wife entered the courtyard with a jug of water.

"Hello. I brought the gypsy kid over. Your turn to look after it," said Mohammad Hajji Mostafa's wife.

"I'm not well. I have palpitations. I can't move. How am I supposed to take care of it?" Saleh's wife said.

"Well, if you can't, tell your daughter to mind it or tell Saleh."

"Maybe you could keep it one more day."

"Absolutely not! You've no idea what we went through last night."

"What?"

"Around midnight two gypsies came to the house and asked for water. We thought they were the kid's parents. But they took off without the kid. Right then the kid woke up and started pacing about. We were petrified. It kept pacing around the room. The house bobbed like a launch on water, tossing us about."

"And what did you do?" Saleh's daughter said.

"We kept calling each other. I was calling Hajji, he was calling his son, then I was calling both of them," said Mohammad Hajji Mostafa's wife.

"And what did the kid do?" asked Saleh's wife.

"It kept pacing around the room in circles," said Mohammad Hajji Mostafa's wife.

"What do you think brought this about?" said Saleh's daughter.

"I think it was the gypsies," said Mohammad Hajji Mostafa's wife.

Suddenly they fell silent. The sound of musical instruments and of women ululating came from the shore.

7

In the evening, Kadkhoda, Mohammad Hajji Mostafa, and Saleh took the child to Zahed, who was sitting in the dark outside his shack, chewing *kiliya*.

"Hey, Zahed, we've brought you a visitor," Kadkhoda called aloud.

"That's nice of you. Good evening! Welcome!" Zahed said.

"A trouble-free guest that doesn't eat, and doesn't need too much room to sleep," Saleh said.

"Whoever it is and whatever it's like, the guest is dear to me like the apple of my eye," Zahed said.

"But this guest is very very young," Kadkhoda said, pushing the child toward Zahed.

"No problem, Kadkhoda," Zahed said.

He sat the child in his lap, took some *kiliya* from the sack and offered it to the men.

"Won't you have some?" he said.

Saleh took some, squeezing it behind his cheek.

"May your honor increase," said Mohammad Hajji Mostafa.

The men walked away hurriedly. Zahed turned to the child, whose eyes glittered brightly, illuminating its small face. The child frowned.

"Why are you frowning? Don't you like me? Well, never mind. Nobody likes me. You'll have to put up with me for the night. You are like me. Why did you come to this world anyway? Why? To go hungry? To sleep in shacks? To consort with spirits? To beat the drum for the possessed and the crazed?"

The child rose.

"I'm boring you, aren't I? Where are you going? Stop! It's dark everywhere and I don't have a lamp to light for you."

The child began to walk away from the cottage. Zahed ran after it, his arms spread open.

"What do you want to do? You want to get lost? To hurt yourself in the dark? Or to fall into the Ayyub reservoir and drown? Don't do it as long as you're my guest. What will I be able to say to people? That I couldn't look after a tiny guest?"

The child sat on the ground. Zahed sat right in front of it and they stared at each other. A strange sound came from the reservoir—the sound of something thrashing about in the water.

"It's a terrible night. Do you hear that? Come, let's go inside."

The child rose, but suddenly dashed toward the reservoir. Zahed followed, grabbing at every shadow and shouting.

"Where are you going? What are you up to? Stop! Stop a minute! I'll give you bread. I'll give you water. I'll give you candy. I'll adopt you as my child. Stop! Stop!"

Near the reservoir Zahed leaped and grabbed the child. From the reservoir came a shriek of laughter.

"You don't know what you're doing," Zahed said, panting. "Let's go to the shack. Do you want me to play the drum? How about the bongo drum? You don't want me to play the drum? Promise you won't run away again. Otherwise I'll have to tie you up and put you in the big drum and hang you in the dark."

8

At noon, Zakariya was sitting in his room under the ventilation tower, mending his fishing net. When Mohammad Ahmad Ali called him, he stuck his head out of a low hole in the wall.

"Come in," he said. "What brings you here this time of day?"

Mohammad Ahmad Ali removed the cloth wrapped around his head.

"I came to see what you're up to," he said.

"Just mending the net."

"Let me give you a hand."

Zakariya pushed the other end of the net toward Mohammad Ahmad

Ali and gave him some thread.

"Zakariya," Mohammad Ahmad Ali began, spreading the net over his knees.

"What is it, Mohammad Ahmad Ali?"

"At noon in the mosque they all refused to take the kid home."

"So what are they going to do with it?"

"Nothing. Let it run loose in the village."

"I can't blame them. The kid messed up their houses, left their lives in shambles."

"And what am I to do?"

"What do you want to do?"

"If they let the kid loose, it's bound to come to my shack at night."

"How do you know?"

"I know, Zakariya. It's bound to come to my shack."

"Well, what do you want to do?"

"I can't stay in the shack. I want to go out to sea."

"What will you do there?"

"I will sleep in Mohammad Hajji Mostafa's rowboat."

"The weather is bad tonight. The sea is rough."

"I have no choice. I can't sleep in the mosque. I'll become possessed if I do."

"Stay with Zahed."

"I can't, Zakariya. He gets up at midnight and beats the drum."

"In whose house do you want to sleep, then?"

"I can't go to anybody's house. Maybe you could let me stay here. I'll stay up all night in the bath and mend your net."

"All right. Stay here tonight. I'll fix you the waterpipe and you don't have to mend the net. Only, go to sleep quietly and don't yell and scream."

"I promise I won't even weep tonight."

9

At sundown, Mohammad Ahmad Ali returned to Zakariya's and hid in the bath. Saleh Kamzari and Kadkhoda took the child to the entrance of the mosque, dropped some candy in its lap, and sneaked away as it was busy eating. A few moments later, the door of every house was shut.

It was a rough, clamorous night; something churned the sea. The child rose and walked to Kadkhoda's house and scratched on the door. Kadkhoda and his wife had been waiting behind the locked door. They began to pray. Disappointed, the child walked to Mohammad Hajji Mostafa's house. Mohammad Hajji Mostafa's wife, who was behind the door, cursed the child and tried to scare it away. The child then went to Abd al-Javad's door. From the roof, Abd al-Javad's mother called her son through the ventilation hole. He went to the roof and emptied a pail of water over the child.

Then a strange clamor rose over the village, as if the earth under the houses was being churned out.

In Zakariya's bath, Mohammad Ahmad Ali lay terror-struck, pressing his face to the floor.

The beat of Zahed's bongo drum rose behind the Ayyub reservoir.

10

In the morning, the child was discovered in Mohammad Ahmad Ali's shack and taken to the entrance of the mosque. Abd al-Javad went after Kadkhoda and Mohammad Hajji Mostafa. It was cloudy and the sea was again noisy. The villagers gathered before the mosque.

"Nobody slept a wink last night," said Zakariya.

"Slept! We nearly died of fright," said Kadkhoda.

"We've got to get rid of the kid right away," said Zakariya.

"Blame all this mess on Saleh. He brought the kid to the village," said Abd al-Javad.

"I didn't do it alone. Kadkhoda's son was with me," said Saleh.

"How were we supposed to know? We thought it was an ordinary kid," Kadkhoda's son said.

"We've got to take it to the desert and leave it there," said Abd al-Javad.

"That's cruel. Wild beasts will kill it," said Kadkhoda.

"They won't. This kid is demonic. Nothing will happen to it," said Mohammad Ahmad Ali.

"I agree with Abd al-Javad. Come on, Saleh. Take the kid. Let's go to the gypsies' route and leave it in their path," said Zakariya.

Saleh took the child in his arms and the men followed, leaving the village behind. The sea had grown more clamorous. A low wind scattered dust upon the road. The men walked in silence, taking turns carrying the child.

They turned round the hills and reached a salt plain.

"This is the gypsies' route," said Zakariya.

"Let's leave it here, then," said Saleh.

They put the child down and left a sack of sweets beside it. It sat motionless, gazing at the plain. Zakariya signalled to the men, who quietly withdrew and turned around the hill.

"Let's go faster," Abd al-Javad said, and the men sped up.

They had covered quite a distance when Zakariya looked back.

"Hey, it's following us!" he exclaimed.

The men looked back. The child was striding toward them.

"It's coming. What shall we do?" said Mohammad Hajji Mostafa.

"Let's change direction. It'll follow us and lose the way to the village," said Saleh.

The men changed their course, clambering up the hill beside the road. When half-way up, they stopped to look down. They could see the child approaching the village with long, quick strides, having absolutely ignored them.

Now the skies were bright. Cheerful sounds bubbled in the sea. Fearful, the men huddled together, staring down apprehensively at the village below them.

FIFTH STORY

Suddenly the sea hushed and the waves ebbed. A cool breeze blew over the motor launch from the north. The men broke off their lively conversation to listen. Something heavy was passing them by deep in the sea, lighting up the water a pale orange.

A few moments later the sea resumed its motion and the waves rolled. Certainly something had come and gone. The men becalmed a moment, then set forth once more, secure in the dark ring that enveloped them. No moon. The gloom weighed heavily over the men and their launch.

"What was that?" inquired Mohammad Hajji Mostafa, who was sitting near the brazier, smoking a waterpipe.

"Whatever it was, it's gone now," said Zakariya, who was sitting at the helm, watching the sea.

"Nothing important," said Kadkhoda's son.

"Whatever it was, it passed by down below," added Saleh, who was squatting over the boxes of cargo.

"Thank God!" said Kadkhoda.

"Since it's good and gone, let's not talk about it," said Mohammad Ahmad Ali.

"Yes, let's keep mum, unless we want to frighten Mohammad Ahmad Ali to death," said Abd al-Javad.

"You won't frighten me to death," retorted Mohammad Ahmad Ali.

"Hey, Zakariya, Mohammad Ahmad Ali doesn't get scared any more. He's grown all guts," Abd al-Javad said.

"No, I haven't grown anything at all," Mohammad Ahmad Ali said.

"So you're still a coward?" said Abd al-Javad.

"Leave me alone, Abd al-Javad, and don't look at me like that," said Mohammad Ahmad Ali, drawing back.

Saleh Kamzari and Kadkhoda's son laughed.

"What's the matter with you two?" Mohammad Ahmad Ali said.

"Stop laughing. Can't you see he's scared?" Abd al-Javad said.

"I'm not scared," said Mohammad Ahmad Ali.

Saleh burst out laughing. Mohammad Ahmad Ali stopped his ears with his hands, put his head on his knees and began to tremble.

"Didn't I tell you he's scared? Didn't I?" said Abd al-Javad.

"It wasn't Saleh's laughter that scared me. Something laughed out there in the sea," said Mohammad Ahmad Ali.

"Don't tease him so much," said Kadkhoda.

Something boomed near the launch and a dark mass emerged from the waves. The men jumped to their feet and followed it with their eyes as it sped by the launch and disappeared.

"What was that, Zakariya?" said Saleh Kamzari.

"It looked weird, Saleh. I couldn't tell," said Zakariya.

"The sea is full of weird things. Don't think about it. You don't have to know what it was. Let's recite the *salavat*,"* said Kadkhoda.

Mohammad Hajji Mostafa and Mohammad Ahmad Ali recited the *salavat*. The men remained silent for a while. Tiny waves besieged the launch, flapping their wings as they rolled ahead. Now and then something would spring out of the water and dive in again. At times, an eye would glitter in the dark and watch the motor launch; then the eyelid would shut.

"Next trip, may it please God, the moon will be showing and we'll have light," said Mohammad Hajji Mostafa.

"I hope so," said Kadkhoda.

"But next trip you won't be around. You're here now because this is the launch's maiden voyage," said Kadkhoda.

"Yes, this time we all had to come," said Kadkhoda.

"After this trip, it will be Zakariya, his motor launch, and endless trips," said Kadkhoda's son.

"May God be his succor. We have always imposed on him," said Kadkhoda.

"Everybody has put his hope on this launch, may God bless it. With the help of the Prophet, finally our village too got to own a launch," said Mohammad Hajji Mostafa.

"May it please God, we won't go without work and food in the summer any more," said Saleh Kamzari.

"I hope so," said Mohammad Ahmad Ali.

"We've got to find a scribe to copy the *panj tan*** to hang in the engine

---

*A benediction in Arabic. Translated, it means "Oh God, bless Mohammad and his descendents."

** The Five Holy Ones, i.e. Mohammad, Fatemeh, Ali, Hassan, Hossein.

room," said Kadkhoda.

"That's a good idea. In Band Mu'allem* this is what everybody who buys a launch does. I've seen it," said Mohammad Hajji Mostafa.

"Hey, look up there!" Zakariya exclaimed.

Over their heads was a patch of cloud with thin ribbons streaming from its borders.

"Do you see that?" said Zakariya.

"It's a cloud," said Abd al-Javad.

"I don't think so. Where could a patch of cloud've come from? Besides, what's it doing looming over our heads?" said Mohammad Ahmad Ali.

"If it isn't a cloud, what is it?" said Kadkhoda's son, his legs dangling down the trap door which led to the engine room.

"It's hard to tell. It could be a cloud, or it couldn't be," said Saleh.

"It's moving. Did you notice?" said Zakariya.

"Yes, over the eddy there's always a patch of cloud like this. Sea captains believe it draws the boats into the whirlpool and sinks them," said Mohammad Hajji Mostafa.

"Maybe it has drawn us too; maybe we're near the eddy," said Mohammad Ahmad Ali.

The men looked behind them. A dark mound was slowly rising from the water.

"O Prophet Mohammad!" Mohammad Ahmad Ali exclaimed.

The launch suddenly lost headway, although the engine continued to run.

"What did you do to it?" Zakariya called aloud, turning to Kadkhoda's son.

"I was sitting up here. I didn't touch the engine, didn't do anything," said Kadkhoda's son, now standing on the deck.

The men were alarmed.

"O merciful God! We're trapped!"** said Mohammad Ahmad Ali, moaning.

Zakariya cautiously released the helm and got up.

"Stop moaning a minute. Let's see what's going on," he said.

The men huddled together. The sea fell quiet around them once more. In the distance, the heavy mass moved along under the sea.

"I don't think we're near the eddy," said Mohammad Hajji Mostafa.

---

* Name of a port town.

** In the original, "giriftar shudim." This is a technical term used in Sa'edi's *Ahl-i Hava* to refer to possession by a supernatural force.

"Then what's this mound? Isn't there a hill near the eddy?" said Mohammad Ahmad Ali.

"There's a shrine and a palm tree on that hill. I don't see any shrine here," said Mohammad Hajji Mostafa.

"Maybe there is one. It's too dark to see," said Abd al-Javad.

"If it is the eddy, what in heaven are we going to do?" said Mohammad Ahmad Ali miserably.

"If you kept quiet a minute maybe I could think of something," said Zakariya.

"God bless you, Zakariya. Hurry up! I'll shut up, won't say another word," said Mohammad Ahmad Ali.

"Let somebody light the big lantern," said Zakariya.

Kadkhoda's son fetched the lantern and Kadkhoda and Mohammad Hajji Mostafa lighted it.

"What next, Zakariya?" asked Saleh.

Zakariya held the lantern over the side and bent over, searching the water as he circled the launch's deck.

"Can you see anything?" asked Kadkhoda.

"No," said Zakariya.

"Just water," said Mohammad Ahmad Ali.

"Then why isn't the launch moving? Maybe there's something wrong with the engine," said Abd al-Javad.

"The engine is fine," said Kadkhoda's son.

"God bless you, Zakariya, take a look at it yourself," said Mohammad Hajji Mostafa.

Zakariya lowered his legs down the opening and jumped into the engine room. Kadkhoda's son followed. Abd al-Javad handed him the lantern and then everyone gathered around the door and stared down. Zakariya had bent over the engine and was listening. The rest of the men huddled around the opening, watching him anxiously.

"Hey, Zakariya, anything wrong with it?" asked Kadkhoda.

"It looks fine, doesn't seem like anything is wrong with it," said Zakariya.

They heard a strange sound, the sound of something being sucked in by the water. The hull swayed gently. The men jumped to their feet. The launch advanced slowly, then suddenly gained tremendous speed.

"Hey, Zakariya! Zakariya!" Kadkhoda and Mohammad Ahmad Ali shouted together.

Zakariya and Kadkhoda's son rushed out of the engine room. Zakariya ran to the helm, grabbing the tiller. But the position of the tiller had no effect on the direction of the boat. Something was spinning and pulling the launch, while a second force pushed the stern up and down.

"We're done for! We're done for!" Mohammad Ahmad Ali groaned.

"What are you doing, Zakariya?" asked Abd al-Javad.

"I'm not doing anything. It's moving on its own. Something is pulling us," said Zakariya.

"Pulling us where? Pulling us where, Zakariya?" said Mohammad Ahmad Ali.

"I don't know. I don't know where," said Zakariya.

"Why are you standing there? Think of something," Abd al-Javad yelled at the men.

"Zakariya has got to decide," said Kadkhoda.

"Turn the engine off," said Zakariya.

Kadkhoda's son who had come on deck, jumped down into the engine room and turned the engine off, but the launch continued at high speed.

"Zakariya, it's still moving," said Mohammad Hajji Mostafa.

"Drop the anchor! Drop the anchor!" Zakariya shouted.

Abd al-Javad and Kadkhoda's son cast the main anchor. The launch jerked and stopped. The men broke out in a sweat. Kadkhoda's son fetched the big lantern from the engine room and carried it to the deck. The men gathered together. Suddenly behind them there was the sound of laughter. The men turned, petrified.

"What was that?" Saleh Kamzari asked.

"A Black. I saw him. He rose from that direction, laughed, and dove back into the water," said Mohammad Ahmad Ali.

2

After some time, the waves subsided and the black cloud assumed the shape of a large bull, its legs folded under its heavy body. Kadkhoda and Mohammad Hajji Mostafa were sitting next to the boxes, smoking the waterpipe. Mohammad Ahmad Ali stood on top of the boxes, while Kadkhoda's son and Zakariya paced the deck. Abd al-Javad was watching a hill nearby from whose summit sometimes flashed a red light. Mohammad Ahmad Ali thought that Blacks in the shrine were smoking a waterpipe.

"I think everything is set now. We can start," Zakariya said to

Mohammad Hajji Mostafa and Kadkhoda.

"Wouldn't it be better to wait until dawn?" said Kadkhoda.

"No, it wouldn't. Zakariya knows what he's talking about. It's much better to start now," said Mohammad Ahmad Ali.

"Why is it better?" said Abd al-Javad.

"I think we'd better start, too. No use staying here," said Saleh Kamzari.

"He's right. We've got to reach Maghviyeh by noon. People will be waiting," Mohammad Ahmad Ali said.

"Turn the engine on," Zakariya said to Kadkhoda's son.

Kadkhoda's son entered the engine room. Moments later the launch jerked and the engine roared. From his perch over the boxes Mohammad Ahmad Ali jumped on to the deck. Zakariya sat with his back to the men, facing the sea and holding the helm. Kadkhoda's son and Abd al-Javad walked to the anchor, took hold of the rope and began to turn the wheel. After a few moments the anchor emerged, its arms tangled in clumps of rope and rags and tied to a long chain the other end of which was in the water.

"Hey, Zakariya, there's a chain tied to our anchor," Mohammad Ahmad Ali shouted.

Zakariya turned to look. Abd al-Javad pulled the chain over the flukes and tossed it into the water. Suddenly the launch jerked and set forward with incredible speed. Strange sounds enveloped them. The boat was spinning like a top.

Zakariya was holding the helm with both hands and Kadkhoda's son and Abd al-Javad were dropping the boxes on to the deck to prevent them from falling overboard. Saleh Kamzari was running this way and that, shifting the boxes around to keep the vessel balanced.

Mohammad Ahmad Ali lay on the deck, his face pressed against the boards.

"Hey Zakariya! Hey Zakariya!" he called repeatedly.

"We're in the eddy! We're in the eddy!" Zakariya shouted.

They were convinced that they were trapped in the countercurrent.

3

At dawn, something burst deep in the water. The launch came to a stop as the sun's crescent rose over the sea. The men had spent the night hanging on to the deck's railings and the boxes. They remained motionless for a moment, then opened their eyes, soaked, too tired to move.

"Is everybody all right?" Kadkhoda asked, without raising his head.

"I'm not all right. I'm dying," Mohammad Ahmad Ali moaned.

Zakariya rose from the helm, walked to the entrance of the engine room and sat down. There was a mild breeze and the sea was calm. Abd al-Javad looked at the sea.

"We've got to be in the eddy," he said.

The others turned to look at the hill which had risen amidst the water, its summit dotted with holes which every few moments emitted a thick smoke.

"That's the shrine. A black *imam* is buried there. He hates sailors. He hates anyone who attempts to cross his territory," said Mohammad Hajji Mostafa.

"It's all Zakariya's fault. He went the wrong way," Saleh said.

"If you all knew it was the wrong way, why didn't you say something?" Zakariya said.

"You had the wheel, not us," said Abd al-Javad.

"Don't blame Zakariya. It was too dark to see," said Kadkhoda.

"I kept saying let's wait until dawn, but no one listened," said Mohammad Hajji Mostafa.

"People will be waiting for us in Maghviyeh at noon," said Zakariya.

"So what? It was our first time on this route. You should've been careful," said Saleh Kamzari.

"It was senseless to buy the launch in the first place," said Mohammad Ahmad Ali.

"Why senseless? Don't other villages buy them? Doesn't every village have a launch? Some have three or four. They work and never go hungry," said Mohammad Hajji Mostafa.

"If I'd known we were going to get trapped in the eddy I would've saved my money," said Abd al-Javad.

"None of us knew that, Abd al-Javad. If we did, none of us would've put money down," said Kadkhoda.

"No use crying over spilled milk. Think of something. Think of a way out of the eddy," said Kadkhoda's son.

"We've got to get out no matter what," said Saleh.

"I think we should save the cargo first," said Kadkhoda.

"Wrong! When a boat is sinking, the crew throws everything overboard to lighten the boat and save their lives," said Abd al-Javad.

"Our situation is different, Abd al-Javad. This is our first trip. If we don't deliver the cargo safe and sound, that's the end. People won't trust us again," said Kadkhoda.

"God bless you, Kadkhoda. You're sensible," said Mohammad Hajji Mostafa.

"Why won't they trust us? We haven't cheated them out of their goods," said Abd al-Javad.

"True, but they may think our launch is unlucky. Then where will we be?" said Kadkhoda.

"What about your lives? You think only about the launch and people's property. Our safety should come first, shouldn't it?" said Kadkhoda's son.

"Excellent. You're right. First us," said Mohammad Ahmad Ali.

"We've got to save our lives as well as the cargo and the motor launch," said Kadkhoda.

"You can't have everything. We've got to see what the eddy is after— us, the launch, or the cargo," said Mohammad Hajji Mostafa.

"I hope it isn't after me. I hope to God it isn't," said Mohammad Ahmad Ali.

"I hope it isn't after any of us," said Mohammad Hajji Mostafa.

"Shouldn't we get going, Zakariya?" said Abd al-Javad.

"I don't think we should," said Zakariya.

"What do you want us to do then?" said Mohammad Hajji Mostafa.

"Someone can take the skiff and row it away from the launch. If we fail to get out of the eddy, he can row to the village and tell them what happened," said Zakariya.

"God bless you, Zakariya. That's a great idea. I couldn't think of anything better," said Kadkhoda.

"Who should take the skiff?" said Mohammad Hajji Mostafa.

"I wouldn't mind going. I like to row," Mohammad Ahmad Ali said.

"If anyone is to go it should be the older men, not you," said Mohammad Hajji Mostafa.

"We need two strong men who can row well and won't get tired or lost. I think Saleh and Abd al-Javad should go," said Zakariya.

"Let's get started, then," said Abd al-Javad.

Saleh Kamzari and Abd al-Javad walked to the stern and lowered the skiff into the water. They stepped into it gingerly and picked up the oars, carefully rowing away from the launch. The rest of the men watched them from the deck.

"Hey, Abd al-Javad, we're going to make a go of it. If we can't make it out of the eddy, rush to Maghviyeh and come back with a rowboat," Zakariya shouted.

"May it please God," said Saleh Kamzari.

"Turn the engine on," Zakariya said to Kadkhoda's son.

"First say *bismillah,** then turn it on," said Mohammad Hajji Mostafa.

Mohammad Ahmad Ali sat cross-legged, his head in his hands. Zakariya took the helm and directed the launch away from the countercurrent. The engine groaned, then roared.

"Shall we start?" Kadkhoda's son stuck his head out of the engine room.

"Yes," said Zakariya.

Kadkhoda's son disappeared into the engine room. Suddenly the launch jerked violently and began to move erratically at incredible speed. Abd al-Javad and Saleh Kamzari rowed with quick strokes and guided the skiff out of the eddy. A countercurrent circled the hill as smoke bellowed from the holes in its summit. Mohammad Ahmad Ali and Kadkhoda's son suddenly yelled something and the launch disappeared behind the hill.

"I swear they won't last the hour," said Abd al-Javad to Saleh.

"God forbid," said Saleh.

They rowed, hurrying to reach Maghviyeh, now and then looking behind them. The motor launch would emerge from one side of the hill and disappear behind the other at dizzying speed.

"I feel sorry for Zakariya," said Saleh.

"Keep rowing, Saleh. We'll be late," said Abd al-Javad.

The sun had risen above the water and was moving toward them. A cold wind blew from the north. Dancing dolphins were chasing the skiff playfully.

---

*These are the first two words of the formula "In the name of God, the Merciful, the Compassionate," recited before beginning a task.

4

Just before noon, Saleh Kamzari and Abd al-Javad spotted the coast.
The scattered palm trees and the vague silhouettes of houses dotting the
shore came into view and disappeared with the fall and rise of the waves.
The two men were exhausted but they continued to row hurriedly. The sea
was rough. The sun blazed over their heads. Now and then large turtles
would swim toward the boat, dividing the water with their supple claws,
stretching their long, lean heads out of the water and pointing in an
unknown direction, before they would vanish under the boat.

The turtles abandoned the skiff when it reached the shore. A large
rowboat was in the water nearby. Some men on its thwarts were watching
the sea. On the shore several men squatted in the shade under the
mosque's portico.

"Though they're looking at the sea, they can't see us," said Abd al-
Javad.

"The sun won't let them. The sea is acting like a mirror. They can't see
a thing," agreed Saleh.

Abd al-Javad let go of the oars, cupped his hands around his mouth
and yelled.

"Hey! Hey!"

A few men rose to their feet in the large rowboat to look their way.

"Hey!" somebody shouted from the portico.

Those in the rowboats jumped out quickly and rushed to the portico.

"Hey!" Abd al-Javad shouted.

Several men from the portico shouted back briefly.

"They're scared. They can't tell who we are," said Saleh Kamzari.

"Faster! Faster!" said Abd al-Javad.

They rowed with rapid strokes until they reached the empty rowboat.
They rested for a moment; then Abd al-Javad gathered up his loincloth
and Saleh Kamzari tied the skiff to the rowboat. The men jumped into
the water and swam to the shore, where they were surrounded by a dozen
villagers carrying sticks. An old long-haired Black was beating the drum on
a roof.

Abd al-Javad and Saleh stepped back nervously.

"Who are you?" asked an old man who was carrying a long stick.

"We aren't strangers. We're from Zakariya's boat," Abd al-Javad said.

"Whose boat?" asked a man wearing wire-rimmed spectacles.

"Zakariya's boat. We come from Zakariya's boat," said Saleh.

"They're lying. Zakariya is still at sea," said a Black who stood behind the spectacled man.

"Zakariya's boat's been trapped in the eddy since last night. We came in the skiff to tell you," said Abd al-Javad.

"How do we know you're telling the truth?" said the spectacled man.

"We're telling the truth, but you don't want to believe us," said Abd al-Javad.

The men looked at each other and lowered their sticks.

"We came to tell you that unless you do something quickly, everything you've got on that boat will sink," said Saleh.

The men stood silently under the scorching sun.

"What are you waiting for? Maybe we can rescue the launch if we start now; otherwise it will sink and ruin us all," said Abd al-Javad.

"I don't think they're lying. We'd better go," said the spectacled man.

The men dropped their sticks. A few rolled up their loincloths and hurried to their rowboat. Abd al-Javad and Saleh Kamzari joined them. A man who wore a leather chin guard offered Saleh and Abd al-Javad a jug of water. Saleh drank first, and before he had passed the water to Abd al-Javad the rowboat was on its way.

The beat of several drums from various directions bade them farewell.

5

The wives of Kadkhoda and Mohammad Hajji Mostafa had built a small shack on the shore. Zahed sat in the middle of the shack, with two drums and several incense burners, surrounded by the old women. The children were gathered outside. The boats had long pulled ashore; the sea was empty. The weather was fine and the sun had risen over the sea. Now and then the water would turn black half way to the horizon, and the children would shout, "Fish! Fish!"

Zahed had placed a handful of *kiliya* in the middle of the floor. Periodically, he'd put a pinch into his cheek and spit on the floor between his legs. Saleh Kamzari's wife had brought a waterpipe and Zakariya's wife had left a small heap of wild rue seeds* in a corner. Kadkhoda's wife had

* It is a custom to burn wild rue seeds to ward off the evil eye.

built a big fire outside, ready to start the *ash-i nazri** as soon as the motor launch appeared.

Just before noon an old black woman came to the shack and greeted Zahed.

"Any news?" she asked.

"Not yet," answered Zahed.

The old black woman bent down and put some *kiliya* on her tongue.

"They're not going to show up for a while," she said.

"They might. They might get here today, or tonight," said Kadkhoda's wife.

"May it please God, they'll be here soon and make everyone happy," said Mohammad Hajji Mostafa's wife.

"What do you think, Zahed?" Saleh Kamzari's wife asked.

"Heaven knows when they'll get back. Maybe today, maybe tomorrow," Zahed said.

"May it please God, it will be as you say," said Kadkhoda's wife.

"It would be nice if Zahed could copy the *panj tan*. We could hang it to the prow of the launch," said Saleh's wife.

"There's no need for that. God himself will protect the launch," said Mohammad Hajji Mostafa's wife.

"Will they take us along on the boat?" Saleh's daughter asked her mother.

"Of course they will. Next week they'll take us all to the pilgrimage of Elijah to pray and to sacrifice a goat, so the sea will be kind to us," said Kadkhoda's wife.

"Too bad I can't go. If I go to sea, I'll start imagining things," said Zahed.**

"Don't go then, stay here," said Kadkhoda's wife.

"Mohammad Ahmad Ali will stay with you, so you won't get bored," said Saleh Kamzari's daughter.

"Trusting in God, I never get bored. When I'm alone, I think of the Blacks and I rejoice," said Zahed.

"May God give you good health," said Kadkhoda's wife.

"May God give you a long life," added Mohammad Hajji Mostafa's wife.

"May your honor increase," Zahed repeated shyly, chewing *kiliya* and nodding.

---

* Thanksgiving stew.
** In the original, "khiyalati misham."

6

The sun had just reached the top of the hill when the countercurrent and the motor launch stopped turning. The men, soaked in sweat, were grasping the deck, moaning. Since the departure of the skiff, they had been turning in the eddy. Mohammad Ahmad Ali had curled up in a corner in the engine room. Zakariya had held on to the helm, and Kadkhoda's son had shifted the boxes around to balance the boat.

"Where's Mohammad Ahmad Ali?" Zakariya asked after a few moments, letting go of the helm.

"I'm here, Zakariya. In the dark," Mohammad Ahmad Ali called plaintively from the engine room, then stuck his head out of the opening.

"What the hell do we do now, Zakariya?" Kadkhoda asked.

"I don't know. I can't think of anything," said Zakariya.

"Let's eat something before it starts again; otherwise we'll perish," said Mohammad Hajji Mostafa.

"And after that we'll say our prayer and make entreaties to God and the Prophet," said Kadkhoda.

"Absolutely not! We shouldn't pray in the eddy, unless you want the Black to fly into a rage," said Mohammad Hajji Mostafa.

Thick smoke bellowed from the holes in the hill.

"Don't talk about him. Don't bring up his name," Mohammad Ahmad Ali pleaded, trembling.

They heard the sound of laughter. Kadkhoda's son spread the dining cloth in the middle of the deck.

"I don't want to die here. I'd die anywhere but here in the eddy," said Mohammad Hajji Mostafa, stumbling over the cloth.

"I don't want to die anywhere at all, Hajji. I'm scared," said Mohammad Ahmad Ali, who had climbed to the deck.

"If we die, the village will turn upside down. No one will believe I'm dead, or Zakariya or Kadkhoda is dead," Mohammad Hajji Mostafa said.

Mohammad Ahmad Ali began to cry.

"Don't cry, Mohammad Ahmad Ali. No one has died yet," said Zakariya.

"Nothing is going to happen. It looks like it's just teasing us," said Kadkhoda's son.

"It's all fate. Nothing we can do about it. We may die here, or we may live. May God have mercy upon our souls and forgive us. May he reward us in the next world," said Kadkhoda.

"We haven't died yet, Kadkhoda. *If* we die, may God have mercy on our souls," said Zakariya.

"You're right, Zakariya. You spoke well. May it please God, it will be as you said," Mohammad Ahmad Ali said.

Zakariya made a big sandwich and stepped aside. Kadkhoda and Mohammad Hajji Mostafa sat down at the cloth. Mohammad Ahmad Ali and Kadkhoda's son did not come to eat.

"Why aren't you two eating?" said Kadkhoda.

"I have no appetite, no appetite at all. The only thing I want is to have solid ground under my feet again," Mohammad Ahmad Ali said.

"Do you suppose Saleh and Abd al-Javad have reached Maghviyeh?" Kadkhoda's son asked Zakariya.

"Heaven knows. Maybe, maybe not," said Zakariya.

"I hope they get back before it starts again," said Kadkhoda.

"There they are! There they are!" Mohammad Ahmad Ali exclaimed. The men looked back and saw a black speck on the horizon.

"They're coming," Mohammad Hajji Mostafa said.

"May God be thanked!" Kadkhoda exclaimed, lifting his arms to the sky.

The men stood up and watched. As the speck moved closer a jet of water shot into the air.

"A whale! There's a big whale coming our way," Mohammad Ahmad Ali said, sneaking down into the engine room.

Several massive whales were approaching the eddy.

7

The sun was in the west when the hill came into view. The sea was rough and the men could hear the countercurrent thundering and spinning around in the distance. Now and then, from the holes in the hill thick smoke rose to the sky. The black cloud had reappeared above the eddy. When they approached the eddy, they saw no sign of the motor launch.

"They aren't there, Abd al-Javad," Saleh Kamzari shouted.

"We're too late. We're ruined," said Abd al-Javad.

"You think the launch's sunk?" asked the man who was wearing a leather chin guard.

"Looks like it," said Saleh Kamzari.

"Maybe they got out," said an old man holding an oar with both hands.

"How? How could they get out of here?" said Abd al-Javad.

"It could happen," said a bearded man sitting on an empty cask.

"I don't think so. If they'd gotten out we would've seen them," said Abd al-Javad.

"You didn't lie to us, did you?" the spectacled man stared at Saleh and Abd al-Javad, who exchanged glances nervously.

The oarsmen let go of the oars and watched them.

"There they are! There they are!" Saleh exclaimed.

The motor launch emerged from behind the hill, carried by the swelling waves. The men rushed to the prow of the rowboat to watch. The launch passed them by, swaying, as large and small waves winged about it in a circle. They saw the shadow of several men lying on the deck, rolling this way and that with the motion of the launch.

"Hey! Hey! Hey!" Abd al-Javad and Saleh shouted, their hands cupped around their mouths.

Muffled voices responded.

"What shall we do?" said the man in the leather chin guard.

"We'll have to wait until it slows down," said Abd al-Javad.

They waited. The motor launch sped by them several times, disappearing behind the hill. Each time, pleading voices called to them for help, until the sun reached the sea, the sky changed color, and something moved on the sea bed. The countercurrent ceased to turn. The motor launch spun a few more times, then stopped.

"Hurry up!" Abd al-Javad said.

The men grabbed the oars and pushed forward. A few moments later they were alongside the launch. Zakariya, who lay behind the helm, raised his head. His face had shrunk, his eyes were sunken, his head seemed smaller than before. He looked at the rowboat for a few moments, then rose slowly. Saleh boarded the launch.

"Is everybody all right?" he asked.

Kadkhoda and Mohammad Hajji Mostafa, who were lying on the deck, rolled over and faced Saleh. Mohammad Ahmad Ali was in the engine room, moaning.

The spectacled man and the man with the leather chin guard climbed onto the deck.

"Are the boxes all right?" asked the old man who stood in the prow, holding an oar.

"Yes, don't worry," said Kadkhoda's son, who was sitting at the foot of the boxes.

"Hey, Abdollah, first bring the boxes," said the bearded man who sat on a cask.

The oarsmen boarded the launch hurriedly and moved the boxes into the rowboat.

"Are you taking the boxes only? Aren't you going to take us?" said Mohammad Ahmad Ali, who had climbed out of the engine room.

"We'll take you too," said the spectacled man.

Mohammad Ahmad Ali ran toward the rowboat.

"Get up, Kadkhoda. Let's save our lives before it's too late," Mohammad Hajji Mostafa said, half rising.

Kadkhoda rose slowly, his hands over his head. He leaned against his son, who walked him to the boat.

"Hey, Zakariya, get in before it's too late," Saleh called from the rowboat.

"What about the motor launch?" said Zakariya.

"Your life comes first," said the spectacled man.

"We sold everything we had to buy this launch. You expect me to leave it to the sea to save myself?" said Zakariya.

"You can't do anything single-handed," said Saleh.

"Why not? Didn't I hold the helm the whole time and keep the boat out of the whirlpool?" said Zakariya.

"What do you want to do now?" said Mohammad Hajji Mostafa.

"I've got to stay here," Zakariya said.

"What should we do?" Mohammad Hajji Mostafa asked.

"Fetch two rowboats. We'll tie the lauch to them. Maybe we'll be able to pull her out," said Zakariya.

"So you're going to stay?" asked Mohammad Ahmad Ali.

"Yes, I've got to stay," said Zakariya.

"Do you have drinking water?" said the spectacled man.

"Yes," said Zakariya.

"What about bread?" said the man.

"Bread, too," said Zakariya.

"Do you need anything? Tobacco? *Kiliya?*" asked the bearded man sitting on a cask.

"No. Just hurry back," said Zakariya.

The men rowed. The boat turned and moved away from the launch. The men looked at Zakariya, who picked the jug of water, went to the prow, and took the tiller. The launch was lighter and floated higher, as if on a translucent, slippery surface.

The sun set as the rowboat disappeared in the distance. From the depths of the whirlpool, a strange beat rose ominously, like Zahed's drum which echoed behind the graveyard on Fridays.

8

At sundown a big launch appeared over the sea. Saleh's daughter and the old black woman, who were sitting on Abd al-Javad's roof, climbed down, shouting, "They're here! They're here!"

The villagers rushed out of their houses and ran to the shore. The large launch loomed over the horizon, moving closer to the village.

Saleh's wife went to the shack and awakened Zahed, who grabbed his largest drum and ran to the edge of the water. Seeing the launch, he jumped up and down and beat the drum. The women and children were cheering and clapping, chanting "Ya Allah! Ya Allah!"

"Wonderful! They came just in time," Mohammad Hajji Mostafa's wife said, clapping happily.

"We'll celebrate all night. No one will sleep," said Saleh's wife.

With the help of the black woman, Kadkhoda's wife lit the fire in the hearth and poured some salt into the cauldron.

Zakariya's wife was dancing and ululating past the line of villagers, distributing chunks of rock candy.

"Calm down! You'll wear yourself out and won't have any energy to sing and dance when the men arrive," said Mohammad Hajji Mostafa's wife.

"No, we won't get tired," said Zakariya's wife.

Zahed beat the drum, jumping up and down on the sand around the crowd, barefoot.

The motor launch came closer and stopped at a short distance from the shore. Zahed put the drum down. The women cheered and waved. A few dolphins surfaced around the motor launch, dancing. The children smiled and quieted down.

"Maybe we should send them a rowboat," said Kadkhoda's wife.

The villagers stepped closer. Strangers clad in black were sitting on the deck. They rose and lined up along the deck to watch the villagers.

"Who are those people?" said Mohammad Hajji Mostafa's wife.

"They look so tall," said Kadkhoda's wife.

"They don't talk. They don't say anything," said Zakariya's wife.

"Zahed, who do you think they are?" Saleh's wife asked.

"Some people dressed in black," said Zahed.

"What are they up to?" asked Saleh's wife.

"I don't know what they're up to," said Zahed.

"Do you know them?" Kadkhoda's wife asked.

"I don't think so," said Zahed.

"I'm afraid! I'm afraid of them!" Saleh's daughter said.

"Don't be afraid. Let's see what they're up to," said Zahed.

A few minutes later the engine roared, the launch made a turn and disappeared in the horizon before the sun had set.

9

The sun had risen when the rowboats reached the hill. The eddy had eased off, slowly circling the hill. The motor launch was nowhere to be seen. The weather was fine and the sea calm. A few sea birds which had accompanied the rowboat for some time circled overhead noisily.

"We're ruined! The launch has sunk. Zakariya has drowned," Kadkhoda said.

"We lost Zakariya for nothing. We shouldn't have let him stay," Saleh said from the other rowboat.

"We're ruined. We lost everything we had. We're penniless," said Mohammad Hajji Mostafa.

"Poor Zakariya! Poor Zakariya!" said Abd al-Javad.

"Do you want to go back now?" asked the spectacled man.

"The sooner the better," said Kadkhoda.

"We'd better go round the hill just once. Maybe the launch is on the other side," said Saleh.

"That's a good idea," said Mohammad Hajji Mostafa.

The rowboats moved to the other side of the eddy in tandem.

"Look! Look over there!" Abd al-Javad shouted after they'd covered a short distance.

Zakariya was drifting nearby, hanging on to a piece of driftwood. Kadkhoda's son jumped into the water and helped Zakariya get into the boat. The man with the leather chin guard gave him water.

"Hey, Zakariya, what happened? What happened?" Mohammad Hajji Mostafa asked, sitting opposite Zakariya and grabbing him by the shoulders.

"She sank," Zakariya opened his eyes.

"Then how come you didn't sink?" said Mohammad Hajji Mostafa.

"It didn't want me. It was after the motor launch," Zakariya said, closing his eyes and falling asleep.

"Hurry up. Let's go," Kadkhoda said.

"Which way?" asked the bearded man sitting on a cask and smoking the waterpipe.

"To our village," said Mohammad Hajji Mostafa.

The bearded man nodded and the rowboats began to move.

10

Just before noon a motor launch with red and black pennants on both sides and strange figureheads in front and back sped by the rowboats. People dressed in black had lined up on deck, watching the rowboats intently.

A trumpet sounded in the launch. The people in black were happily speeding toward the eddy.

SIXTH STORY

Late at night Mohammad Ahmad Ali left Zahed's shack. Zahed was suffering from colic. Zakariya had sent Mohammad Ahmad Ali to fix him a decoction and to rub his stomach with ointment. When Zahed fell asleep, Mohammad Ahmad Ali helped himself to a handful of *kiliya* from Zahed's bag and went outside. The evening wind had subsided and it was quiet everywhere. The moon, small and red, was suspended over the Ayyub reservoir.

Mohammad Ahmad Ali stopped for a moment and watched the date palms in Mohammad Hajji Mostafa's orchard. They stood side by side in a row, with drooping branches. Mohammad Ahmad Ali took a few steps toward the reservoir, then stopped.

"It's quiet everywhere," he thought. "It looks like something is going to happen."

He put a pinch of *kiliya* behind his cheek.

"I'd better not get close to the reservoir," he decided. "When it's quiet like this something is bound to happen."

He walked back, went around Zahed's shack and started for the shore. Near the water he looked behind him. The moon had grown smaller and redder and was circled by a dark ring. Mohammad Ahmad Ali began to walk along the shore, taking long steps toward his home. After a few minutes, fear possessed him again.* He stopped and took a few deep breaths. He watched the sea cautiously. Suddenly he saw a dark mass motionless against the horizon. Fear filled his heart. He waited a few moments. From the far distance came the sound of something being cut, and a few streaks of light issued from the dark mass, illuminating the water.

Mohammad Ahmad Ali began to run toward the village, yelling and screaming. He heard the voices of a few men speaking behind the walls but continued to run. He dashed from one alley into the next until he

---

* In the original, "giriftar shud," a term used in *Ahl-i Hava* to refer to the state of possession by a supernatural force.

reached Zakariya's house and began banging at the door.

"Hey! Hey, Zakariya!" he yelled.

"Hey, Mohammad Ahmad Ali!" Zakariya's voice came from the ventilation tower.

"Come out here! Come out, Zakariya," cried Mohammad Ahmad Ali.

"What the hell is it again?" Zakariya's voice came from the ventilation tower.

"Come out! Come out, Zakariya!" Mohammad Ahmad Ali pleaded.

"What's wrong with you again?" Zakariya asked through the ventilation tower.

"Come out! Come out," said Mohammad Ahmad Ali.

"Has something happened to Zahed?" Zakariya asked.

"Come out here," Mohammad Ahmad Ali said.

A few figures emerged from the dark. Kadkhoda's voice was heard from the next alley.

"Hey, Mohammad Ahmad Ali, God damn you for raising a hullabaloo again," he said.

"I'm not raising a hullabaloo; I'm just scared," said Mohammad Ahmad Ali, now calmer.

"What are you scared of this time?" asked Mohammad Hajji Mostafa, who was standing behind Mohammad Ahmad Ali.

"I wish you'd die of fright and leave us in peace," said Kadkhoda's son.

Zakariya appeared with a lantern.

"Is something the matter with Zahed?" he asked.

"No, Zahed is all right. There's something out in the sea," said Mohammad Ahmad Ali.

"Why, were you out at sea?" Zakariya asked.

"No, I saw it on the way here," said Mohammad Ahmad Ali.

"Didn't you agree to stay with Zahed?" said Zakariya.

"I left after he fell asleep," said Mohammad Ahmad Ali.

"Couldn't you have put your carcass down to sleep there?" asked Zakariya.

"He went to sleep with his eyes open. I couldn't stay on," said Mohammad Ahmad Ali.

"What made you walk back along the shore? You could've come by the path behind the reservoir," said Kadkhoda.

"I couldn't. The reservoir was too quiet," said Mohammad Ahmad Ali.

"You're afraid of everything. You're afraid if there is noise; you're afraid if there is no noise. You're afraid if there is wind, and afraid if there is no wind. You're afraid at night and afraid during the day. You don't let us get a good night's sleep," said Kadkhoda's son, laughing.

"I swear, you would've been scared too if you were in my place. That thing is still in the sea. If you don't believe me go and see for yourselves," said Mohammad Ahmad Ali.

"All right. Come along. Let's go see what's in the sea," said Zakariya.

The night was darker and over the Ayyub reservoir the moon burned with small violet flames.

Zakariya and Mohammad Ahmad Ali began to walk toward the sea and the rest of the men followed them. They passed the small square opposite the mosque, went round Saleh Kamzari's house, and reached the high sand hill behind it. From the hill the villagers could view the entire sea. They climbed the hill and saw, on the horizon, a dark mass with a few floodlights that illuminated the water in several directions.

"Do you see that? Now do you believe me?" said Mohammad Ahmad Ali, his voice trembling.

They stood silent, watching.

"What can it be?" asked Kadkhoda.

"It seems to be still. It isn't moving," said Mohammad Hajji Mostafa.

"It's probably a foreign launch and they've stopped to have a smoke from the waterpipe," said Saleh Kamzari.

"It's much bigger than a launch. It looks like a ship," said Zakariya.

"Where is it from?" said Saleh.

"Not from the eddy, I hope," said Abd al-Javad.

"O Mohammad, Messenger of God!" Mohammad Ahmad Ali exclaimed.

"I hope it hasn't come from the eddy," said Kadkhoda.

"What is it doing in our waters?" asked Mohammad Hajji Mostafa.

"I don't know. But so far they haven't bothered us," said Zakariya.

"What do you think we should do?" asked Kadkhoda.

"Nothing. Let's just go back and get some sleep. In an hour we'll have to go out to sea and cast our nets," said Zakariya.

"It's not wise to leave," said Saleh.

"I agree. It's not safe. It's not even safe to go out to sea before it leaves," Abd al-Javad said.

"Why?" asked Zakariya.

"Something could happen," said Abd al-Javad.

"He's right, Zakariya. For God's sake stay. Let's see what happens," said Mohammad Ahmad Ali.

"They're right, Zakariya. We'd better wait," said Kadkhoda.

And they all sat on the hill and waited.

2

Dawn came and the ship became visible. Long and stately, she lay on the water. On deck, people rushed about. The village men were still sitting on the hill; their women and children stood on the shore, waiting. Kadkhoda's son and Saleh were on Saleh's roof, watching the sea, which was changing color.

"Hey! Hey!" Saleh cried suddenly.

"What is it?" Kadkhoda asked.

"They're coming this way. Launches coming this way," said Saleh.

"O Merciful God! I knew this was going to happen," said Mohammad Ahmad Ali.

"Let them come. We'll see what they're up to when they get here," said Zakariya.

"Hey, Saleh! How many launches are there?" asked Kadkhoda.

"I can see three clearly," said Kadkhoda's son.

"He's right. I can see three too," said Abd al-Javad, who was sitting beside Mohammad Hajji Mostafa.

They all stood up and watched.

"Who do you think they are?" asked Mohammad Hajji Mostafa.

"I have no idea," said Abd al-Javad.

"I hope they aren't going to harm us," Kadkhoda said.

"What do you think we should do?" asked Mohammad Hajji Mostafa.

"We must wait," said Zakariya.

"You mean we should just sit here and do nothing?" Abd al-Javad said.

"We don't know what they're up to yet. We won't know until they get here," said Zakariya.

"What if they get here and we find out they've got something up their sleeves?" Mohammad Hajji Mostafa said.

"Like what?" asked Zakariya.

"Like plundering our groves," said Mohammad Hajji Mostafa.

"You mean to say with all this to do they've come to plunder our groves?" said Zakariya.

"Could be. It's happened before, hasn't it Kadkhoda? Now forget the groves, what if they want to plunder our homes, or beat us up, or kill a few? Then what?" said Mohammad Hajji Mostafa.

"I hope they haven't come to draft us into the army. If they have they'll take us all," said Abd al-Javad.

"We'd better leave the village," said Mohammad Ahmad Ali.

"Where can we go?" asked Mohammad Hajji Mostafa.

"Some place where they can't catch us," said Mohammad Ahmad Ali.

"Are they still coming, Saleh?" Kadkhoda yelled, looking up.

"Yes, and they're in a rush besides," said Saleh from the roof.

"Hey, Kadkhoda, if they try to hurt anyone, we've got to stay together and stop them," said Mohammad Hajji Mostafa.

"Good idea. That's what we should do," said Kadkhoda.

"What if they wanted to do something to me?" asked Mohammad Ahmad Ali.

No one responded.

"They've slowed down. They're very close," Kadkhoda's son called from the roof.

"The women and children should go home. Go to your homes," Mohammad Hajji Mostafa shouted at the women.

"Hurry up, quick. Take the children home," Kadkhoda yelled.

The women quickly disappeared in the alleys.

"What about us? Shouldn't we leave too?" Kadkhoda said.

"We'd better gather in the mosque," Mohammad Hajji Mostafa said.

"I'm not leaving. I'll stay here to see what happens," Saleh said.

"I'll stay too. I'll stay with Saleh," said Kadkhoda's son.

"If something happens, let us know," Mohammad Hajji Mostafa said.

The men hurried past Saleh's house to the small square. Saleh Kamzari and Kadkhoda's son lay down on the roof and peered at the launches approaching the shore on the clear sea.

3

Kadkhoda's son entered the small square, panting. The men, who had gathered in front of the mosque, rose to their feet.

"What happened?" Mohammad Hajji Mostafa asked.

"They changed direction and went to the far side of Salem Ahmad's house. They're landing," said Kadkhoda's son.

"Do you suppose they plan to come to the village from that direction?" Kadkhoda asked.

"I don't think so. I think they're going to stay there," said Kadkhoda's son.

"Stay there? Stay to do what?" asked Zakariya.

"I don't know what they're up to. But they have brought more stuff than you could imagine," said Kadkhoda's son.

"What sort of stuff?" Zakariya asked.

"A dozen tents, some big chests, and lots of odds and ends," said Kadkhoda's son.

"Who are they? What are they like?" Mohammad Hajji Mostafa asked.

"I don't know who they are. Some Blacks and some strange looking people wearing different kinds of hats and colorful clothes," said Kadkhoda's son.

"Aren't they Arabs?" Mohammad Hajji Mostafa asked.

"No, they're not. They're not from the Islands either. I couldn't tell where they're from. Anyway, they're minding their own business," said Kadkhoda's son.

"What happened to the launches?" asked Kadkhoda.

"They went back to the ship. I don't think these people are going to bother us. Saleh said you can go watch them from his roof if you want to," said Kadkhoda's son.

"Well, if they aren't going to bother us, we can go and watch them," said Zakariya.

The men started for Saleh's house.

"Still, it's better if they don't see us," said Mohammad Hajji Mostafa.

"Why?" Zakariya asked.

"Prudence. Things could change suddenly. Besides, they might want to trick us," said Mohammad Hajji Mostafa.

"Whatever you say. You can do as you please, but I'm not scared of being seen," Zakariya said.

They reached Saleh's house. Zakariya crossed the alley and climbed the sandy hill. Abd al-Javad climbed the sandhill too. Kadkhoda and Mohammad Hajji Mostafa entered Zakariya's courtyard and quietly climbed up the ladder to the roof. Saleh was all eyes, sitting on the roof and staring at the other side of Salem Ahmad's house.

"Hey, Saleh! What are you looking at?" Mohammad Hajji Mostafa asked.

"Them," said Saleh, laughing.

"Why are you laughing, Saleh Kamzari?" said Kadkhoda.

Saleh did not answer. Kadkhoda and Mohammad Hajji Mostafa raised their heads. A short distance from Salem Ahmad's house, several men wearing different kinds of hats were pitching tents. They were running around, hard at work. The tents were multi-colored. Several brass chests set on the shore glittered in the morning sun.

Zakariya called Mohammad Hajji Mostafa from the top of the hill. "Hey, Hajji, it doesn't look like they've come to plunder you. They've got everything they need," he said.

"Then what do they want here?" said Mohammad Hajji Mostafa.

"I don't know. Heaven knows," Zakariya said.

"They may have mistaken this for some other place," Kadkhoda said.

"You may be right," said Zakariya.

"Maybe they want to hunt around here. What do you think, Kadkhoda?" said Abd al-Javad.

"Excellent! It must be as you say. They've come to do some hunting," said Kadkhoda.

"Hey, look!" Kadkhoda's son exclaimed, pointing toward the sea. They all turned. Some more launches were approaching the shore. In the front launch were big colorful umbrellas under which stood people wearing sunglasses; in another, men wearing straw hats sat on large chests.

"Damned if I lie. Something is up," Saleh called out from the roof.

"I don't think it's something bad," Zakariya said from the top of the hill.

"Looks like they plan to stay here for a while," Saleh said.

"They can stay as long as they want to, provided they leave us alone," said Mohammad Hajji Mostafa.

The launches stopped at a distance from the shore. A few Blacks appeared from the now erected tents with a large litter and waded out to the big launch. The men shaded by the umbrellas sat in the litter and leaned back against the railing around it.

"I'll go see where they've come from," said Zakariya.

No one said anything. Zakariya walked toward the strangers' camp.

4

Around sundown, the villagers gathered in front of Salem Ahmad's living room. No one was left in the village. The men in front and the women and children behind them were squatting, watching the strangers. Mohammad Ahmad Ali was sitting behind Zakariya. No one had taken the news to Zahed, yet there he was, lying on the side porch of the living room, watching the tents.

A cool breeze blew from the sea. From the hills on the other side of the shore, the sinking sun cast a large shadow over the tents.

Inside an enormous tent, food was being prepared in large pots. Several Blacks were lifting the lids and inspecting the contents. They wore white aprons and had wrapped white handkerchiefs over their mouths. Outside the tent, fish was being fried over the hearth. Behind the tent, a few men were sawing something. From the tent in the middle, came the sound of men and women laughing.

"What delicious smells, Kadkhoda," said Zahed, who was lying on the porch.

"Yes, I guess they're having a party tonight," said Kadkhoda.

"They're lucky. They can eat all they want," Zakariya said.

"The smell of tuna and pepper is driving me mad," said Mohammad Hajji Mostafa.

"I wish they'd give us some. I wish we could eat, too," the women clamored.

"I am so hungry I'd eat all the food if they let me," said Mohammad Ahmad Ali.

"What do you think they're making?" asked Abd al-Javad.

"They'll make whatever they want. I swear they're also making tuna fish," said Mohammad Hajji Mostafa.

"I hope they're making rice, too," said Mohammad Ahmad Ali.

"We'd better leave. Sitting here won't do us any good. We won't get anything," said Kadkhoda's son.

"I couldn't bring myself to leave," Kadkhoda said.

"Me, too. I haven't seen so much food in a long time," said Mohammad Hajji Mostafa.

"These smells intoxicate me; they make me hungry," said Mohammad Ahmad Ali.

"Me, too," said Mohammad Hajji Mostafa.

"You don't still think they want to do you in, do you Hajji?" asked Zakariya.

"No, not any more," said Mohammad Hajji Mostafa.

"I wish we could say a couple of words to them," Kadkhoda said.

"If we'd gone over at the start and greeted them, maybe we would get something tonight," said Mohammad Hajji Mostafa.

"It isn't too late; we can still go over and greet them," said Saleh.

"I don't think they know our language," Zakariya said.

The sound of a strange musical instrument came from the tents. The villagers fell silent and listened.

"Do you hear that, Zahed?" Abd al-Javad turned to Zahed.

"Yes, I hear," Zahed said, sitting up and nodding.

"What kind of instrument do you think it is?" Mohammad Ahmad Ali asked.

"I think these people are *hava'i,*"* said Zahed.

"How come they don't play the drum then?" asked Zakariya.

"They aren't from the sticks; they don't like drums," said Zahed.

A child began to cry. Kadkhoda looked at the women and shouted angrily, "Shut him up!"

A woman went to the child. The crying stopped.

Several tall men opened a large table in front of the tents. Some of the Blacks set a large number of dishes on the table.

"I swear they're going to start," said Mohammad Ahmad Ali.

"Yes, they're going to eat; they're going to eat," said Saleh.

"Good! Good! It'll begin now," said Abd al-Javad.

"They're the ones who are going to eat, so what are you so cheerful about?" said Zakariya.

"Why shouldn't we be? Nothing wrong with eating, is there?" said Mohammad Ahmad Ali.

"I, for one, like to see how they eat," Saleh said.

"That's simple. They'll take some food, put it in their mouths, and chew," said Zakariya.

"I hope so. I hope they eat to their hearts' content," said Mohammad Ahmad Ali.

"Mohammad Ahmad Ali, you'd better shut up and stop fidgeting so much, so we can see what the hell they're up to," said Kadkhoda.

From the tent, the Blacks brought large dishes of food to the table. The wind had calmed down. It was getting darker, when suddenly a motor roared and the tents were suddenly lit up.

"Greetings to Prophet Mohammad," said Mohammad Ahmad Ali. A few of the villagers recited the *salavat* quietly.

"I guess they want to stay up all night," Zakariya said.

"Let them stay up, Zakariya; let them do what they want," said Kadkhoda.

A bell rang. The Blacks who surrounded the table stepped aside. Then three women came out of the tents. They were tall and wore colorful clothes. The women did not wear veils; their hair fell to their shoulders.

---

*i.e., people who believe in possession by supernatural powers. Playing music, especially the drum, is part of their ritual.

"Their women! Take a look at their women!" Mohammad Ahmad Ali was beside himself.

"Marvelous! Marvelous! Can you see that, Kadkhoda?" Mohammad Hajji Mostafa said.

"Hey, Zahed! Can you see them? Can you see the women?" said Mohammad Ahmad Ali.

"Yes, I can. I envy those men," said Zahed.

"I bet they're a lot of fun, the women; aren't they, Zahed?" said Mohammad Ahmad Ali.

"I guess so," said Zahed.

"They're as smooth as smelt," said Mohammad Ahmad Ali.

"And so white!" said Saleh.

"I bet they taste good, too," said Zahed.

"I envy their men," said Abd al-Javad.

"They'll eat first, then take the women into the tent, hold them between their legs and do it on and on and on, until the sun rises," said Mohammad Ahmad Ali.

"What's that to you, Mohammad Ahmad Ali? You won't be doing any of it," said Zakariya.

"I know. I don't want to do it," said Mohammad Ahmad Ali.

"But I do. I swear I want to do it, too. I like to do it with women," said Saleh.

"Who doesn't, Saleh? Everybody likes it," said Kadkhoda.

"Woman is a great gift, first food then woman," said Mohammad Hajji Mostafa.

The six men and women were standing around the table, laughing.

"I swear to God Almighty these are important people. You'll see," said Kadkhoda.

The men and women sat around the table and began to eat.

"I can't see too well from here. I'm getting a bit closer," said Saleh, moving a few steps closer as he was sitting.

"Saleh is right; we can't see too well from here," Zakariya said moving next to Saleh.

"I think I'll move closer too," said Mohammad Hajji Mostafa, moving next to Zakariya.

"In that case, I will, too," said Abd al-Javad.

Before long, all the villagers had moved closer to the tents.

"Can you see them well now, Saleh?" asked Mohammad Hajji Mostafa.

"I'd see them better if I were closer," said Saleh, moving a few steps closer to the tents as he was sitting. The others followed suit.

"Saleh is quite right. We'd see better if we were closer," Zakariya said. They all moved closer still.

"Let's not get too close. They may not like it if they see us," said Kadkhoda.

"Why shouldn't they like it? We aren't going to eat their food. We'll just have a peep at them," said Zakariya.

"That's right. We'll have a peep. That's all. Nothing to get excited about," said Mohammad Hajji Mostafa.

The villagers crawled forward.

"I swear to the *Imam** I want to get right to the table. I can't restrain myself," said Saleh Kamzari.

They moved closer until they were only a few steps from the table, which was covered with various dishes. The strangers were sitting at the table, talking and laughing. Now and then, they would take some food to their mouths.

"I wish I could have a taste of that," said Mohammad Ahmad Ali.

Suddenly one of the women turned and saw the villagers. She jumped to her feet and gasped, startled. The others too rose from the table. The villagers huddled together in terror and waited, their eyes full of fear.

5

By the time they returned to Salem Ahmad's house it was late at night. They set the large cauldron of food in front of the parlor door. Kadkhoda pushed the courtyard door open and motioned to the women, who stood behind him, to enter. The women and children rushed into the courtyard.

"Open the parlor door to get the food in," said Mohammad Hajji Mostafa.

Mohammad Ahmad Ali opened the parlor door and they carried the food inside. The room was dark and smelled of ashes everywhere. The men returned to the stairs.

"We need light," Kadkhoda said.

"I'll take care of that," said Saleh.

He went into the courtyard and a few moments later returned with a burning lantern. Once again all the men entered the kitchen. Saleh hung the lantern on the wooden hook near the hearth. Then they dragged the

---

* The twelfth Imam, who is invisible. Shiites believe that he will return to earth to save mankind.

cauldron into the light. Zakariya bent over one of them and looked inside.

"I can't tell what's in the food," he said.

Mohammad Ahmad Ali put his hand in the cauldron and took a bit of food.

Mohammad Ahmad Ali put his in the cauldron and took a bit of food.

"Let me eat this. Maybe I'll be able to tell what it's made of," he said.

Mohammad Hajji Mostafa became angry.

"Let nobody touch the food," he shouted.

"Restrain yourselves a little. Let's see how we should do this," said Kadkhoda.

"If these people aren't Moslem, we can't eat their food," said Mohammad Hajji Mostafa.

"Why can't we? What has food got to do with whether they're Moslems or heathens?" said Zakariya.

"We can eat it. We can eat it fine," said Mohammad Ahmad Ali.

"I hope they're all Moslem. Would they've given us all this food if they weren't? said Kadkhoda.

"Hey Mohammad Ahmad Ali, did it taste good?" said Saleh.

"I don't know what it tasted like. But if you people let me I'll eat a thousand more morsels," said Mohammad Ahmad Ali, licking his fingers.

"If you eat a thousand morsels, there won't be any for us," said Mohammad Hajji Mostafa.

"Yes, it's for everyone. Everybody must get to eat. If anybody doesn't want his share, he can give it away," said Kadkhoda.

"If anyone gives me his share, I'll pray to God to reward him a thousand times in the next world," said Zahed.

"Keep your reward. I'd rather eat my share," said Zakariya.

The women outside thrust their arms through the parlor window, clamoring.

"What's the matter? Be quiet a minute. Let's see what we're doing," Mohammad Hajji Mostafa said.

The women stepped back, grumbling.

"Leave them alone, Hajji. They're hungry. They want to eat," said Kadkhoda's son.

"Eat what? We've got to divide it up first," said Mohammad Hajji Mostafa.

Mohammad Ahmad Ali spread his headcloth on the floor.

"Put my share in this," he said.

Saleh laughed and the rest of the men spread their cloths on the floor.

"Who'll divide up the food?" Zakariya asked.

"You do it, Zakariya. You're good at it and you're fair," said Kadkhoda.

Zakariya rolled up his sleeves.

"All right. Since you think I'm fair, I will," he said, filling his cupped hands with food and emptying them into Mohammad Hajji Mostafa's headcloth.

"May God grant you a long life," said Mohammad Hajji Mostafa.

"May your honor increase," said Zakariya, filling his cupped hands again and emptying the food in Kadkhoda's cloth.

"Zakariya, your hands were smaller this time," said Kadkhoda.

"It's your imagination. My hands are the same size," said Zakariya.

"Don't grumble, Kadkhoda. Your portion is more generous than mine," said Mohammad Hajji Mostafa.

"I hope Zakariya's hands get enormous when my turn comes," Mohammad Ahmad Ali said to Abd al-Javad.

Abd al-Javad moved his headcloth closer and Zakariya emptied his cupped hands in it. Abd al-Javad tasted the food. ·

"How is it, Abd al-Javad? Tastes good?" asked Mohammad Hajji Mostafa.

"You've got some yourself. Taste it," said Abd al-Javad.

"I can't bring myself to. It's too good to eat," said Mohammad Hajji Mostafa.

Zakariya continued to fill his hands and empty the food in the cloths.

"Don't forget the women and children," said Kadkhoda.

"Is it our fault that we don't have wives and children? Is it, Mohammad Ahmad Ali?" said Zahed.

"We have to eat less because we don't have wives and kids," said Mohammad Ahmad Ali.

The women clamored more loudly. Zakariya looked at them; so did the other men. The women pressed against the open window, sticking their arms into the room, moaning.

"Go home. We'll bring you the food right away, and then you'll eat," Kadkhoda shouted, rising.

"Don't forget the old women," a weak voice said from the dark.

"Have pity on the poor and give them more," said Zahed.

6

Mohammad Ahmad Ali had barely fallen asleep when he heard two people talking outside the shack. He rose and stuck his head out through the straw mats. Abd al-Javad and Kadkhoda's son were walking toward the shore.

"Hey, where are you going?" Mohammad Ahmad Ali cried.

"To the sea, fishing," said Kadkhoda's son.

"It's too early. Isn't it, Abd al-Javad?" Mohammad Ahmad Ali said.

"Yes, it is," said Abd al-Javad.

"Why are you so early, then?" asked Mohammad Ahmad Ali.

"We wanted to chat a bit," said Kadkhoda's son.

Mohammad Ahmad Ali came out of the shack and began to walk beside them.

"Where are you going?" asked Kadkhoda's son.

"I want to chat a bit, too," said Mohammad Ahmad Ali.

"We don't want to chat. We want to go over there to see what's going on," said Abd al-Javad.

"Fine. I'll go with you," said Mohammad Ahmad Ali.

All three began to walk toward the tents.

"I think they're all asleep now," said Abd al-Javad.

"Let them sleep. We aren't going to bother them," said Kadkhoda's son.

"They may get annoyed," said Mohammad Ahmad Ali.

"Don't go with us if you're afraid," said Abd al-Javad.

"No, I'm not afraid," said Mohammad Ahmad Ali.

They hadn't gone more than a few steps when they saw Saleh walking toward Salem Ahmad's house with a stick.

"Hey Saleh, where are you going this time of night?" said Abd al-Javad.

"I'm going to see what's happening over there. Where are you all going?" said Saleh.

"We're going to see what's up, too," said Kadkhoda's son.

"I hope they'll give us something," said Mohammad Ahmad Ali.

"You gorged yourself only two hours ago and you want more!" said Kadkhoda's son.

When they reached Salem Ahmad's house, they found Zakariya, Mohammad Hajji Mostafa and a few more men sitting in front of the house, watching the newcomers' camp.

In the tents, the lights were on. Some of the newcomers were still going about. The men and women were still up, laughing and talking in their tents.

"Why didn't you go home to sleep?" Zakariya asked when he saw the other villagers.

"We came to watch. What about you?" said Saleh.

"We came to watch, too," said Mohammad Hajji Mostafa.

Saleh Kamzari and Mohammad Ahmad Ali sat next to Zakariya, and Abd al-Javad and Kadkhoda's son squatted a few steps ahead of them.

The sea was smooth and clear. The big ship stood on the horizon, its lights on.

"Did you find out what they're doing here?" asked Kadkhoda, who had just arrived.

"God willing, we will soon. We have to be a bit patient," Mohammad Hajji Mostafa said.

"The problem is we can't talk to them," said Saleh Kamzari.

"But many of them know our language; we can talk to those," said Zakariya.

A few moments later Zahed appeared.

"Hey, Zahed, you weren't feeling well. What are you doing here?" Kadkhoda said.

"I couldn't sleep, Kadkhoda. I thought something might happen. They might give you something and I'd get shortchanged," said Zahed.

"Don't worry. Nothing has happened yet," said Mohammad Ahmad Ali.

"You mean to say they haven't given you anything yet?" said Zahed.

"That's right," said Zakariya.

"You expect me to believe that?" said Zahed.

"Suit yourself," said Kadkhoda.

Zahed turned to Mohammad Ahmad Ali.

"Hey, Mohammad Ahmad Ali, if something happens when I'm not here, remind them of the miserable man who's been starving behind the Ayyub reservoir all his life," he said.

"God willing, I will," said Mohammad Ahmad Ali.

A few moments later, the rest of the villagers arrived and sat around Salem Ahmad's house.

"Hey, Kadkhoda, looks like nobody is sleepy tonight," said Zakariya.

"Well, they've got a reason. Of course they aren't sleepy," Kadkhoda said.

"We've got to set out to sea in a few minutes," said Kadkhoda's son.

"I, for one, am not planning to go out to sea tonight," said Saleh.

"Me, neither. I don't want to go out to sea," said Zakariya.

"What will you do tomorrow? What will you eat?" asked Mohammad Hajji Mostafa.

"May it please God, they'll give us something and we won't go hungry," said Zakariya.

"May it please God, they will," said Abd al-Javad.

"God willing. God willing," said Zahed.

"Now that we're not going out to sea, hadn't we better get a bit closer?"

Saleh said.

"Excellent idea," said Mohammad Hajji Mostafa.

The men rose and tiptoed toward the tents.

7

At dawn, a tall black man in a red shirt appeared from the camp and found the villagers huddled together in front of the tents. He paused, then strode toward them. Some of the villagers began to move back.

"Stay where you are; he isn't going to bother us," said Zakariya.

"He's annoyed. You can tell by his looks," said Mohammad Ahmad Ali.

"Don't pay him any attention. Pretend you haven't noticed anything," Zakariya said.

"What do you want here?" the Black asked, when he reached the crowd.

"Nothing," said Zakariya.

"Nothing? This early, you must have come for something!"

"No, we haven't come for anything. We're just sitting here."

"Don't you people have work to do?"

"Not today, we don't have to work today."

"Don't you go out to sea?"

"Sea? No, we don't go out to sea."

"Who does all this fishing gear belong to, then?"

"I guess it belongs to us."

"In that case you do go out to sea."

"Sometimes we do, and sometimes we don't."

"Why didn't you go today?"

"To tell you the truth, we didn't feel like it."

"Why did you come to sit here?"

"We like it here; it's nice."

"Isn't there some other place you like?"

"To tell you the truth, no. We like this place a lot more."

"It's all the same around here."

"You're right. It's all the same."

"In that case, get up and go somewhere else."

"You're very kind. But we're comfortable where we are."

"I know. You came here to look at the tents, didn't you?"

"I guess so."

"Well, you have no business looking at the tents. Get up! Go somewhere else."

"We could be looking at the tents, or we could be looking at the sea, or the sky, or something else," said Zakariya.

"I swear I was just looking at the sea," protested Mohammad Ahmad Ali.

"I wasn't looking at anything," put in Zahed.

"Lies! All lies! I know you were looking at the tents. Get up! Get out of here," cried the black man.

"We won't. We're staying. We aren't bothering anyone," argued Saleh.

"This place belongs to us," added Abd al-Javad.

"No it doesn't. Get up! Go somewhere else. Hurry up! Hurry Up!" shouted the Black.

"We have no quarrel with you, so why are you shouting?" answered Zahed.

"Get up! Get up! On your feet, quick!" said the Black.

"All right. Don't shout. We'll leave," muttered Kadkhoda.

They all got up and slowly walked away. The Black returned to the camp and went into one of the tents. The men stopped and looked back.

"Hey, Zakariya, the Black is gone," said Saleh.

"Let's go back where we were," cried Zakariya.

The men returned and sat where they had been sitting before and gazed at the tents.

"Hey, Zakariya, the kitchen is getting busy again," said Saleh.

"Thank God," said Kadkhoda.

"So much smoke. May it please God they'll cook a lot. May it please God they won't eat it themselves and will give it to us," Mohammad Ahmad Ali said.

"Here they come," Mohammad Hajji Mostafa exclaimed.

Two Blacks in red shirts were standing outside the tents looking at them.

"Don't look at them. Don't look at anything," Zakariya said to the men.

"Not look? How can we do that?" Mohammad Ahmad Ali said.

"Bend your heads down," Zakariya said.

They bent their heads down and closed their eyes. A few moments later the Blacks were standing before them.

"You came back," said the first Black.

"What?" Zakariya raised his head.

"Why did you come back?" said the first Black.

"Come back? Come back from where?" Zakariya said.

"Didn't you leave?" asked the first Black.

"No we didn't leave. We didn't go anywhere. Hey, Kadkhoda, did we go anywhere?" Zakariya said.

"Don't you know you have no right to sit here?" said the second Black.

"No, we don't," said Zakariya.

"Well, now you do. You can't sit here," said the second Black.

"What will happen if we do?" said Zakariya.

"It's obvious. They'll wake up. They won't like that," said the first Black.

"I don't think they'll mind," said Zakariya.

"You'd better get the hell out of here," said the first Black.

"Heaven help you if you don't," said the second Black.

"What if we don't?" said Zakariya.

"Get up! Get up, quick!" the Black shouted.

"All right, don't shout. We'll leave," said Kadkhoda.

"All right. There's plenty of room elsewhere," said Mohammad Hajji Mostafa.

They got up and walked away. The Blacks went back into the tent. The villagers looked back.

"Hey, Zakariya, they're gone," said Mohammad Ahmad Ali.

"What shall we do now?" said Kadkhoda.

"Let's go back," said Zakariya.

They tiptoed back and sat where they had been sitting before.

"O Prophet of God," exclaimed Mohammad Ahmad Ali.

A dozen black men rushed at them, twisting their long whips over their heads. The villagers jumped to their feet and began to run. Near the village, they looked behind them. The Blacks were gone.

"They're gone. They're nowhere in sight," said Saleh.

"They're back in their tents," said Abd al-Javad.

"What shall we do now?" said Mohammad Ahmad Ali.

"Let's go back," said Zakariya.

They joined hands and started for the camps gingerly.

8

Just before sunset, Mohammad Ahmad Ali and Saleh Kamzari went to the mosque.

"What's up?" asked Mohammad Hajji Mostafa, who was sitting before the *mehrab*.

"Good news! Good news!" said Saleh.

"May you always be the bearer of good news! What's happened?" said Kadkhoda.

"Food! Food and lots of it, as much as you like," said Mohammad Ahmad Ali.

"Really?" said Zakariya.

"I swear to God. There's so much food we could eat it for two weeks and not finish it," said Mohammad Ahmad Ali.

"Where is it?" asked Zakariya.

"Heaped up in front of Salem Ahmad's house," said Saleh.

"Then why didn't you bring it along?" asked Kadkhoda.

"It'd take more than one or two men. We all have to go there," said Saleh Kamzari.

"What are you waiting for? Let's go," said Mohammad Hajji Mostafa. They all got up, ready to go.

"We need containers," said Mohammad Ahmad Ali.

"Go to my house and fetch three baskets. Two for me and one for you," Zakariya said to Mohammad Ahmad Ali.

"I'm going to fetch a trough," said Kadkhoda.

"I'll fetch two troughs," said Mohammad Hajji Mostafa.

When they left the mosque it was getting dark and the sea could be heard from all directions. Zahed hastened toward Salem Ahmad's house.

"Hey, wild man, don't you need a container?" Saleh Kamzari asked Zahed.

"No, I'll eat my share there and finish it on the spot," said Zahed.

9

Early in the evening the men had gatherd under the mosque's portico. A big lantern burned in the middle of the small square. Each man had one or two baskets at his side.

"We haven't gone to sea for a long time," said Kadkhoda.

"Yes, it's been long," said Saleh.

"Imagine how many fish we've missed," said Kadkhoda.

"Nobody needs fish now," said Zahed.

"Sure, who needs fish when he's full?" said Mohammad Hajji Mostafa.

"I don't feel like going to sea. I wouldn't go to sea for anything," said Abd al-Javad.

"The sea is for the hungry. Thank God, we're full," said Saleh, rubbing his swollen belly.

"We don't need the sea any more, do we Kadkhoda?" said Mohammad Ahmad Ali.

"I don't know. Maybe you're right, maybe not," said Kadkhoda.

The men could hear the sea in the remote distance.

10

It was late afternoon and the village men who were sitting in front of the mosque saw a few Blacks approaching; behind them were the three men and the three women, being followed by a crowd.

The villagers rose.

"Hey, Zakariya, if they ask any questions, you talk to them," said Mohammad Hajji Mostafa.

"I hope to God they won't ask us anything," said Zakariya.

"What do they want here, Zakariya?" said Mohammad Ahmad Ali.

Zakariya did not answer. The Blacks came nearer. They looked friendly, smiling.

Kadkhoda approached them.

"Welcome! You're most welcome!" he said.

"Ask them what they want here," said Mohammad Ahmad Ali.

Zakariya nudged Mohammad Ahmad Ali, who fell silent and stepped back.

"They've come to see the whole place," one of the Blacks said.

"The whole place? Hey Zakariya, they've come to see the whole place," said Kadkhoda.

Zakariya stepped forward.

"What do they want to see?" he asked.

"Everything," said the Black.

"Like what?" asked Zakariya.

"The whole village, the houses," said the Black.

"Didn't I warn you!" said Mohammad Hajji Mostafa.

Saleh Kamzari nudged Mohammad Hajji Mostafa, who fell silent and backed away.

"Why do they want to see the village?" Zakariya asked.

"No special reason. They just like to see every place," said the Black.

"I mean the houses," said Zakariya.

"They like to see houses too. They want to see how you people live," said the Black.

"Like everybody else," said Zakariya.

"I swear to God we didn't do anything. We're poor, unfortunate people. Let us be," Mohammad Ahmad Ali cried.

"Don't worry. They're not going to harm you. They want to have a look, nothing more. They like places like this," said the Black.

"Besides, if you don't want them to, they won't mind. They'll just leave," said another Black.

"And you'll lose out if they do. You're poor people. Maybe they'll feel sorry for you and give you something; help you out," said the first Black, winking.

Mohammad Ahmad Ali ran forward.

"In that case come to see my house first. I'm poorer than everybody else. I'm destitute. I don't have anything," he said.

"Be quiet for a minute, Mohammad Ahmad Ali. Let Zakariya speak," said Kadkhoda.

"They want to see all the houses. They like strange things," said the Black.

Zahed, who was standing behind the other villagers, stepped forward.

"My shack is stranger than all the houses. I'm a hermit, a wild man; I've several drums. I sing and I've got more than twenty bamboo sticks from India and Muscat," he said.

"They're not looking for bamboo sticks and they don't like drums," said Saleh.

"I'll sing for them," Zahed pointed at the strangers. "I sing well. I've sung for these people a hundred times—more, a thousand times," he said, pointing to the villagers.

"Keep quiet for a minute," Zakariya shouted at Zahed.

One of the women, who had very long hair, stepped forward and asked something of the Black. The Black answered her. The strangers talked together and laughed.

"Hey, Zakariya, what do they say? Why are they laughing?" said Kadkhoda.

"I can't make it out," said Zakariya.

The Black turned to the villagers.

"They say just a few houses would do," he said.

"In that case see my house first," said Abd al-Javad.

He grabbed the Black's hand and dragged him toward his house. The rest followed, turned the corner into the alley, and entered Abd al-Javad's house. In the courtyard, a few fishing nets hung from the wall. There were two terra-cotta bowls and a water jug on the porch. Abd al-Javad's mother was sitting on the roof, grinding wheat in a handmill.

Abd al-Javad stepped ahead of the crowd and opened the door to the room. The rest followed him and looked into the room. One of the women said something and the rest laughed. She entered the room and walked to the mantlepiece, where a few daggers were hanging from the wall. The rest also went in and looked around.

"These are daggers. Good stuff," said Abd al-Javad, removing one from the wall and giving it to the long-haired woman. She pulled it out of the sheath. One of the men said something and the rest laughed and touched the sheath.

"These daggers are very dear to me. Someone brought them for me from the Island," said Abd al-Javad.

The Black turned and spoke to the strangers. The man who was holding the sheath said something to the Black, who then turned to Abd al-Javad.

"Is it for sale?" he asked.

"Of course it is. I'd very much like to sell it," said Abd al-Javad.

The Black laughed and gave some money to Abd al-Javad.

"You finally had your way, Abd al-Javad," said Saleh Kamzari in the back of the crowd.

"I've got two more here. They're fine too. Don't you want to buy them?" Abd al-Javad asked the Black.

Kadkhoda pushed his way through the crowd and stepped forward.

"No, they don't. Don't be so pushy, Abd al-Javad. Shouldn't the rest of us make something, too?" he said, then grabbed the Black's hand. "Let's go to my house. I've got much better things," he said, dragging the Black out of the room.

Everybody laughed. All followed Kadkhoda and the Black. When they left Abd al-Javad's house, Zakariya stepped forward and addressed the crowd.

"Let me tell you right now, so you'll remember. After Kadkhoda's it's my turn," he said.

11

At sunset, it was Zahed's turn. The strangers, accompanied by the villagers, passed the reservoir, and went to Zahed's shack, carrying several rugs, daggers, gunpowder casks, terra-cotta bowls, walking sticks, coffee pots, water jugs, and kerosene lamps. Zahed was walking ahead of the crowd, nodding vigorously.

"This is Zahed's home," he rubbed his hands together, when they arrived at the shack. "Zahed doesn't have daggers or coffee pots, or gunpowder casks. Zahed is poor, but he's got better things. He's got bongo drums, kettle drums, more than twenty bamboo sticks, and good *kiliya*."

He went into the shack and returned with a bag. He filled his hand with *kiliya* and held it before the visitors. They looked at each other, puzzled.

"It's very good. No one has *kiliya* as good as mine. I give *kiliya* to anyone who wants it. I have given *kiliya* to Mohammad Ahmad Ali more than a thousand times. I've given *kiliya* to Saleh and Kadkhoda, to everybody. It's very good. Take some," said Zahed.

He took a pinch and put it behind his cheek and nodded. One of the women leaned over and smelled the *kiliya*. She puckered her lips.

"They don't like this," said the Black.

"All right. If you don't like *kiliya*, I'll show you the bamboo sticks," he said.

He went into the shack and returned with several long bamboo sticks. He held them up before the crowd.

"These are fine bamboo sticks. Very rare. Two of them are from Muscat, the rest from India. They're all good; they've magical properties," Zahed said.

One of the three men motioned to the Black, who gave some money to Zahed, took the bamboo sticks, and tucked them under his arm. The women entered the shack, talking to one another as Zahed displayed his drums.

"These are all mine," Zahed said. "All of them are mine. Zahed is poor. He's a Negro, he's a wild man, but he's got all these drums. Do you want me to play for you?"

The Black spoke to the women. They laughed and nodded yes. Zahed picked a large kettledrum and left the shack. They all gathered around him and he slung the drum over his shoulder.

"Hey, Kadkhoda what shall I play for them?" Zahed said.

"Whatever you like," said Kadkhoda.

"I want to play something good," said Zahed.

"Make up your mind, or they'll leave before you start," said Zakariya.

"I hope they won't. I hope they'll stay and listen, and give something to this poor man. I want to play 'Ya Allah' for them," said Zahed.

" 'Ya Allah' is no good. Play something else," said Mohammad Hajji Mostafa.

"You're right, Hajji. I'd better play 'Moludi' and you can sing along,"

Zahed said.

He spat in his palms, picked up the drumsticks, and began to play, moving his head from right to left, his body moving up and down. Suddenly, a great clamor came from the back of the shack. The crowd looked behind them and saw the village women passing by the reservoir and coming toward them, dancing and playing the tambourine.

12

They reached the ship around midnight. The sea was stormy and they had rowed their boats out to the ship at great effort. A few dim lights burned on the deck, and no sound could be heard from the cabins.

"Hey, Zakariya, what if there's someone on deck?" Saleh said.

"I don't think there'll be anyone," said Zakariya.

"Besides, even if there is someone, it's no problem," said Abd al-Javad.

"How can it be no problem?" said Kadkhoda's son.

"We'll say we have come to see the ship. It'll be all right," said Zakariya.

"And go back empty-handed?" said Abd al-Javad.

"Let's go and see what happens," said Zakariya.

They began to climb the ladder. They heard no sound from the cabins and stepped onto the deck gingerly. There was a strange odor on deck. They walked along the railing and entered a narrow corridor in which two metal doors faced each other. Zakariya stopped, listened carefully, then opened one of the doors. He stuck his head in, then signalled to the others to follow. It was a large cabin with metal studs on the wall. In one corner there were four chests, one on top of the other.

"Hurry up, quick," said Zakariya.

Saleh hauled one of the chests on his back and passed the corridor to the deck. Near the ladder the three caught up with him, each carrying a chest. They descended the ladder carefully and placed the chests in the rowboat. A few moments later they returned to the ship, crossed the deck, and entered the corridor. Zakariya pulled the other door open. The cabin was occupied. A slim black man was sitting on a low cot, smoking a pipe. When he saw the men he smiled.

"There's nothing in here. Just some rope, and a few tin cans over in that corner; I don't think they'll be of any use to you," he said.

"I can use them. I need ropes a lot," said Saleh, who was standing near Zakariya. Saleh went inside, gathered the rope into a bundle and tucked it under his arm. They left the cabin and walked through the corridor to the deck. There, they saw two other Blacks, leaning against the railing, whispering to each other and laughing.

13

Kadkhoda and Mohammad Ahmad Ali entered the kitchen tent with a big cauldron. Some Blacks were sitting on a bench near the fire, smoking pipes.

"Hello, is the food ready?" said Kadkhoda.

"I don't think so," said a Black who wore a white apron.

Kadkhoda went to the fire and lifted the pot-lid.

"Yes it is. It's perfectly ready," he said.

Mohammad Ahmad Ali held the cauldron and Kadkhoda ladled the food into it. He filled the large cauldron and put the lid back on the pot.

"May your honor increase," he said to the Blacks.

"You're welcome," said the Black, laughing.

Kadkhoda and Mohammad Ahmad Ali left the kitchen-tent and approached another tent. Mohammad Ahmad Ali coughed, then stuck his head in. A tall man lay in bed, reading a book.

"Hello, you got anything around here we could use?" said Mohammad Ahmad Ali.

The man shook his head and smiled.

"He's one of those who don't speak our language," said Mohammad Ahmad Ali to Kadkhoda.

Kadkhoda and Mohammad Ahmad Ali entered the tent and looked around. At the head of the bed was a box of candy on a low table. Kadkhoda took the box.

"Good bye," he said to the man.

The man waved. They walked toward the third tent, which was unoccupied, and found a pile of strange household items.

"Hey Kadkhoda, can you make these out?" asked Mohammad Ahmad Ali.

"No, I can't make them out at all," Kadkhoda said, surveying the objects.

"Neither can I. What do you think they are for?"

"Heaven only knows. I've no idea."

Mohammad Ahmad Ali put the cauldron down and pulled out one of the objects. It consisted of a long handle attached to a bowl-shaped part with the wrong side up.

"What do you suppose this is for?" Mohammad Ahmad Ali asked Kadkhoda.

"I don't know. Maybe it's something good; maybe it isn't," said Kadkhoda.

"Yes, I think it's good too. Maybe it is for soup."

"How could you eat soup in it? It'd spill out, wouldn't it?"

Mohammad Ahmad Ali studied the object. He lay the handle on the ground in such a way that the bowl was positioned right side up.

"I think that's what they do. Somebody holds the handle and the rest gather around the bowl and eat the soup," he said.

"Excellent! You're right," said Kadkhoda.

"I like it. I'll take it."

He took the object and the cauldron and they both left the tent. In the fourth tent two women were sitting at a table, drinking coffee, and a Black was standing before them. Kadkhoda entered the tent.

"Hello, have you got anything around here we could use?" he said.

"Like what?" said the Black.

"Anything. It makes no difference. Pots and pans, clothes, food, cigarettes, anything good. We need anything," Kadkhoda said.

The Black spoke to the women. The women laughed.

"We don't know what you're looking for, so how can we give it to you?" the Black said to Kadkhoda.

Kadkhoda looked around the tent. There was a single slipper on the floor a few steps from him. He bent over and picked it up.

"This is good. I want this. May your honor increase," he said.

The women laughed. Kadkhoda and Mohammad Ahmad Ali went toward the fifth tent.

14

Having finished eating the food out of the cauldrons, the village men got up and, with difficulty, dragged themselves to the mosque's portico, where they collapsed, side by side.

"I can't breathe any more," said Mohammad Hajji Mostafa.

"I'm going to explode. I can't touch my stomach," said Kadkhoda.

"I'm stuffed every inch with food—my stomach, my chest, my arms, my legs, my head, all of me is full of food," said Zakariya.

"I won't get hungry again even if I don't eat for a thousand years," said Zahed, moaning and rolling on the ground.

"I've changed. No one could lift me now. And even if they lifted me, I'd just fall right down again," said Mohammad Ahmad Ali.

"Look at Abd al-Javad. He looks like someone has blown him with air," said Saleh.

"Obviously you can't see yourself. You look like a dead cow," said Abd al-Javad.

"We're all like that. We've eaten so much, we've gotten fat, plump, round," said Zakariya.

"And my house is just like myself, full every inch. So much stuff packed in there!" said Kadkhoda.

"I don't even know what half the stuff I've picked up is for," said Mohammad Hajji Mostafa.

"Everybody's house is like that. We'd better worry about ourselves first," said Zakariya.

"What do you think we should do?" said Kadkhoda.

"We'd better not move. Let's just stay here and see what happens," Saleh said.

"He's right. Getting up may be dangerous. Besides, who could manage to get up?" said Abd al-Javad.

"It's all that fat they made us eat," said Zakariya.

"Then why didn't they themselves get fat like us?" said Mohammad Ahmad Ali.

"It's God's doing," said Zahed.

"No, Zahed. It's not God's doing. They don't eat like we do, do they?" said Zakariya.

"I think if we go on like this we'll all be metamorphosed," said Mohammad Hajji Mostafa.

"How?" asked Saleh.

"We'll stop looking human," said Mohammad Hajji Mostafa.

"O, I'm dying!" said Kadkhoda.

"O, I'm suffocating!" said Zakariya.

"I wish I could purge myself somehow," said Zahed.

"I wish there were a few holes in my body, so some of it could spill out. That would be a relief!" said Abd al-Javad.

They began to moan in chorus. A few moments later the women appeared in the alley. They too had changed. They were fat, round, bloated, rolling on the ground slowly and crawling forward, carrying large wooden spoons in their hands. It took a while before they gathered around the cauldron. Then they began to fill their spoons and empty them down their throats, moaning.

"O Imam! Help me! I've no room any more," said Kadkhoda's wife.

"I wish I had one more stomach; I wish I had two more stomachs," said Mohammad Hajji Mostafa's wife.

"That can't be helped, so let's stop complaining and just eat," said Zakariya's wife.

"She's right. Let's eat. Let's eat," said Saleh's wife.

A few moments later, the women dropped their spoons, lay down near the cauldrons, and began to moan.

"Hey, Saleh, what the hell shall I do? I'm exploding," Saleh's wife cried.

"Bend your knees up and breathe slowly," said Saleh.

"How could I? How could I bend my knees? I'm full every inch. My hands, my legs, my head, my chest, all are full of food. How could I breathe?" Saleh's wife said.

15

Just before dusk, three black men entered the small square, carrying cauldrons of food. The villagers still lay on the ground, their stomachs bloated.

"Hey, what's wrong with you? Get up! Time for dinner," said one of the Blacks.

"Tonight's dinner is something else," said another.

"Tonight's dinner is richer and tastier than ever. Get up! Quick!" said the third Black.

"We can't move. We can't get up," said Mohammad Ahmad Ali from the portico.

"You've got to get up; otherwise it'll get cold and won't taste good," said the second Black.

"Give me a few minutes. I'm exploding!" said Kadkhoda.

"Have pity! Be fair!" said Mohammad Hajji Mostafa.

"No way! We cooked it for you. We can't throw it away," said the Black.

"God's blessings mustn't go to waste," said the third Black.

"Don't worry. We'll eat it all. You can be sure of that. We won't let it go to waste," said Saleh.

"This blasted food of yours sticks to our intestines like lime. It doesn't come out," said Abd al-Javad.

"It's because it's good, nutritious," said the second Black.

"We're all bloated," said Kadkhoda.

"I'm turning into a whale," said Abd al-Javad.

"I've grown bigger than a cow," said Mohammad Ahmad Ali.

"Even four horses couldn't budge me an inch," said Mohammad Hajji Mostafa.

"Have pity on us," pleaded the women.

"This is all true; you've got a point. But what are we to do with the dinner? What?" said the third Black.

"We'll eat it. Just give us an hour," said Saleh's wife.

"Honest?" said the Black.

"Honest, I swear," said Zakariya.

"This isn't a trick?" said the Black.

"What trick? How could you pull a trick about eating or not eating?" said Zakariya.

The Blacks set the full cauldron next to the empty ones and left the small square.

16

A few days later the villagers started for the strangers' camp, holding hands, keeping an eye on one another. All were panting, too obese to take regular steps.

"Hey, Zakariya! Hey, Kadkhoda! Look!" shouted Mohammad Ahmad Ali when they arrived near Salem Ahmad's house.

The tents had been removed and there was no sign of the strangers on the shore.

"What's happened?" said Mohammad Hajji Mostafa.

"They seem to have left," said Zakariya.

They turned and looked at the sea. It was empty. There was no sign of the ship or the launches.

"Where have they gone?" said Kadkhoda.

"I don't know," said Saleh.

"I don't think they've left for good. I hope they'll come back," said Abd al-Javad.

"What are we to do, if they don't?" said Mohammad Ahmad Ali.

"I don't know," said Kadkhoda.

"If they don't we're in a lot of trouble," said Zakariya.

"Poor me, I'm worse off than anyone else here. At least you can go out to sea and fish. I can't do anything," said Zahed.

"Not me, I'm not going to sea," said Saleh.

"Me neither. I don't like fishing any more," said Abd al-Javad.

"I've gotten used to eating good stuff," said Mohammad Ahmad Ali.

"I'm already hungry," said Kadkhoda.

"I want good food, good rich food," said Zakariya.

"I want variety. I don't like soup any more," said Mohammad Ahmad Ali.

"Now that we can't have all kinds of food what are we to do?" said Kadkhoda.

"Let's sit by the sea and wait. Maybe they'll come back," said Mohammad Hajji Mostafa.

They started for the sea, moving their bloated bodies with difficulty. The sea had shrunk. It had ebbed away from the village and resembled a drying swamp. The early morning sun rays were opaque gold against the horizon. A foreign boat with a single black sail wandered over the water, at a loss as to which way to go.

17

Zakariya left Mohammad Hajji Mostafa's storage room. The lights were out and everybody was asleep. A heavy bag on his back, he looked around him, tiptoed across the courtyard, and entered the street. Outside, it was strangely light. The moon was large, burning with purple and violet flames over the Ayyub reservoir.

Zakariya crossed the little square and reached his house. The village was in a deep sleep and darkness enveloped the houses. He pushed the door in, went to the storage room at the other end of the courtyard, left the bag at the door, and returned to his room. He had just lain down when he heard a strange clamor outside. He rushed to the courtyard with a dagger. The door to the storage room was open, and someone was trying to get out.

Zakariya went closer. Saleh came out of the storage room with a large bag.

"Stop! Let me see, Saleh Kamzari. What are you doing here?" said Zakariya.

"Nothing, I was just passing by," said Saleh.

"In my storage room?"

"Yes, I was just passing. I thought I'd just take a look in here."

"What have you got in the bag?"

"Nothing, odds and ends, just junk."

Zakariya raised his dagger.

"I'm going to cut you open right here, so you won't ever dare touch my stuff again," he threatened.

Saleh Kamzari stepped back, threw the bag at Zakariya, and ran out of the courtyard. Zakariya ran after him, shouting. The noise awakened Kadkhoda, who rushed into the bath to get his headcloth. Suddenly he saw Abd al-Javad sitting in a corner, eating.

"Hey, Abd al-Javad, what are you doing in my house?" Kadkhoda said.

"Nothing. I was hungry. I thought maybe I'd find something to eat here," said Abd al-Javad.

"You thought maybe you'd find something to eat here? Why, is this your house?" said Kadkhoda, suddenly attacking Abd al-Javad, who dodged away and ran into the street. Kadkhoda continued to chase him, screaming.

Outside, the village was in a commotion, the men shouting and cursing, the women hurling rocks from the roofs. Zakariya was going in a circle around his house with a dagger.

"If anyone comes this way, I'll spill his guts," he shouted.

Mohammad Hajji Mostafa stopped in front of the mosque and shouted back.

"Hey, Zakariya, my storage room is all empty. I know who did it. Saleh told me. Wait till the sun comes out. Then I'll show you."

In the shadow of the walls, Kadkhoda's son, an old hatchet in his hand, tiptoed toward Mohammad Hajji Mostafa. The moon over the Ayyub reservoir had burned itself out, extinguishing itself in the dark, prolonged night.